BENGAL HOUND

BENGAL HOUND

A Novel

RAHAD ABIR

Published by Gaudy Boy LLC,
an imprint of Singapore Unbound
www.singaporeunbound.org/gaudyboy
New York

For more information on ordering books, contact jkoh@singaporeunbound.org.

ISBN 978-1-958652-02-2 / eISBN 978-1-958652-03-9
Library of Congress Control Number: 2023938029

Cover design by Flora Chan
Interior design by Jennifer Houle

For
Tania & Rafan

A strange darkness has descended on the world these days,
Those who are completely blind claim to see the most;
Those who feel no love—or affection—or the flutter of pity
Have become crucial to controlling the world.
—JIBANANANDA DAS, *A STRANGE DARKNESS*,
TRANS. BY FAKRUL ALAM

Time tells me what I am. I change and I am the same.
I empty myself of my life and my life remains.
—MARK STRAND, *THE REMAINS*

PART
ONE

CHAPTER ONE

1

Her letter arrived on Friday morning. He had sensed it would come one day. There was little he could do now—there was no stepping back.

From the university's English department office, he checked his supervisor's availability. At 12:10, he walked toward room 207. The aroma of tobacco drifted into the corridor. Door ajar, the supervisor was sitting in his chair, puffing on his pipe.

He entered and greeted the professor.

"What is it, Shelley Majumder?" The supervisor took his pipe out of his mouth. He was flanked by two portraits—Shakespeare and Tagore—hanging on the walls.

"My father," he said. "He's gotten ill," he lied.

"I'm sorry to hear that."

"I need a few days off to visit him."

The supervisor put the pipe back in his mouth.

Shelley stared at the professor's teak table and saw an open book. A burgundy tobacco tin next to the book read "Prince Albert."

"Didn't he join your mother and sisters in India?"

"No," Shelley said. "He doesn't want to."

"Your poor father. Loves the scent of Bengal. I understand." He granted Shelley a one-week leave of absence.

—

The bimonthly *Cinemagazine*'s office was on North Brook Hall Road. Shelley had come early today. A few days out of Dhaka meant many tasks would have to be done in advance. To mark the sixth anniversary of her death, the upcoming issue of the magazine was spotlighting Marilyn Monroe, and Shelley had to write the lead story.

He drained a glass of water and focused on the asthmatic ceiling fan that eclipsed the sound of chattering typewriters. He picked a pen, uncapped it, and thought about Marilyn Monroe. Then Marilyn Monroe and Arthur Miller together. When did they get married? Did Miller feel lucky to have her? How did he feel after her suicide? Was he now going to write a play called *Death of a Performer*?

"Shelley!"

He looked up, his pen poised above the paper.

"Are you okay?" the senior editor asked from far across the room.

"Yeah."

"How did you like my cover story last week?"

"Last week?" Shelley tried to remember.

"On Satyajit Ray."

"Ahh. It was phenomenal. Made me want to watch his films."

"Blasphemer!" the senior editor said with his characteristic humor. "Indian films are banned. Did you forget?"

"Doesn't work for me," Shelley said. "I'm an English movie buff."

"More blasphemy! Watch some Urdu pulp, too. Be 'Paktriotic.'"

Throughout the afternoon Shelley worked on his Marilyn Monroe article. For the title he pondered a moment, closed his eyes, and came up with two headlines:

1. *The Final Days of Marilyn Monroe*
2. *The Last Days of Hollywood's Sex Symbol*

The first one sounded fine to him. With the second, orthodox readers might be offended due to the word *sex*. Shelley picked the first title, and then quickly edited two short articles.

By the time he stood up from his desk, it was evening. He was the last person to leave.

2

A smell of evening greeted him as he stepped outside. The mid-August air felt refreshing. He trudged toward Victoria Park. At this hour the park looked eerie. It had a cold, creepy aura. Standing for a while outside the park, he peered at peculiar silhouettes inside, hoping to hear sounds of breathing. It was believed that the dead souls of the hanged, the 1857 sepoy mutineers, were still lingering around those palm trees.

He started down along Laxmi Bazaar and found a rickshaw. He ought to see Manick—the only friend with whom he could talk about the looming crisis he was going to face. The three-wheeler rattled past Dufferin Muslim Hostel, past Holy Cross Church, past the Prince of Wales Bakery, and took a left turn.

He thought of Roxana. A memory came back to him from half a dozen years ago when he was a teenager. One midday he was at his desk, deep into the puzzle of an algebra problem. Roxana's face popped up at the open window, and her hand dropped a fresh shefali flower bracelet on his notebook. He picked it up, sniffed it, and carelessly put it aside. "Dhur! It has no smell."

Her cheery face darkened. She said nothing, but her eyes said she was hurt. She swung away and disappeared.

For over a week she didn't come before him. When he ran into her at school, she looked away. The next day he caught her by the bamboo bush, on the trail she used on her way home from school.

"Hey, what happened? Why don't you talk to me?"

Throwing a glance at him, she hurried her steps.

"Look what I've brought for you." He held out two luscious guavas from his pockets.

From the corner of her eyes, she glanced at his hands, but showed no interest and kept walking. Confused, he watched her in silence. Then something struck him. His mind flashed back to the day she'd given him the flower bracelet.

The following day he waited for her again. When she came holding books to her chest, he opened his palm before her, where lay the shefali flower bracelet, now dry and brown.

"It still smells good," he said.

She gave him a warm look, and her cheeks broke into playful dimples. A deep, dreamy grin. He offered to pluck boroi jujube from Motla's with her. She smiled an agreeable and adorable smile.

About twenty yards away Motla's property started along the trails. They cautiously walked through the bushes and soon stood under an old jujube tree. Spotting countless blushing red borois up in the branches, their mouths watered, for this tree produced the sweetest borois in the neighborhood. Shelley climbed the tree slowly and carefully. Positioning himself at a safe limb between two meeting branches, he carefully held a thin branch, avoiding the thorns. Once he began shaking, borois rained down on the ground. Roxana collected them and threw them into the hem of her frock.

Maybe five minutes passed. There came a shout. "Who's there?" Motla's voice cried from the backyard.

Shelley gingerly moved down.

"Quick," Roxana said.

Five feet off the ground, Shelley jumped from the tree, and away they ran. They stopped at a safe distance under a chatim tree to enjoy the stolen borois. Then Roxana pointed at his left hand.

"You're bleeding."

He looked at the edge of his finger, blood oozing from the cut. He brushed the blood away. "It's nothing."

She held the finger and saw blood oozing again. She popped his finger inside her mouth. He felt the tip of her warm tongue sucking. He looked at her in amazement. As she met his eyes, her face flushed. She brought the finger out of her mouth.

"Let me get some durba grass." From the side of the trail, she pulled some young blades of grass and rolled them between her palms. Then, squeezing the grass strands hard, she applied the juicy ball to his finger.

Shelley smiled to himself. The memory of that day was still fresh in his mind. He sighed after a moment. Those had been the best days of his life. Life was full. The house in Gopala was alive. His sisters, mother, father—a happy family, all under the same roof. A sharp pain stabbed his heart. His family was now broken, cut apart by the bloody borders drawn by the British.

3

The marble plaque on the wall read "Dream Garden." Beneath it the plaster was peeling off. Over the front gate there was an arch of willowy Rangoon creeper, and inside the gate a concrete walkway led to a two-story Bengali-European-style house.

Manick opened the gate to let Shelley in.

"I was just off to your place." Manick shook Shelley's hand.

"Too late."

They walked into the living room. Shelley told Manick about Roxana's letter and his decision.

"Do you think you are doing the right thing?" Manick asked. "During the final year of your degree?"

"It's now or never," said Shelley.

"The responsibility is huge."

"I don't fear the responsibility."

"I bet you don't," said Manick.

"Is that a joke?"

"Of course not. What I'm saying is . . . you are still a student, you have no proper job, and, on top of everything, you will have no family support. From either side."

"I have the magazine job. Plus home tutoring. I can manage. But anyway, I'm trying to switch to a daily."

"Things may not go as easily as you think, Shelley."

Yes, things might not go as he hoped. The political situation was worsening by the day. Student strikes, class suspensions—nothing new. Shelley remembered the 1964 riots. That year he had been supposed to apply to Dhaka University, but had dropped the idea as the country bled from communal violence. The year had been difficult. Their sweet home crumbled as though by river erosion. Shelley was born in the year of the Partition, 1947. But for him, the real Partition took place when the family was divided in 1964. A home torn in two. It was somewhat of a relief for him to move to Dhaka the following year, beginning a new academic phase.

"I know," Shelley said. "I know things will be really tight for a couple of years. But it's possible. After all, we're not making babies now."

Unannounced, Maya entered carrying a tray. A fleeting smile of greeting, then the tray in her hands landed on the table.

"Who's going to make babies?" she asked without looking up. Her hands began unloading the tray. A plate of pineapple biscuits. Two cups of milk tea.

"Maya," Manick said to his sister, "Shelley's going to his village."

"Aha. When?"

"You are off tonight, aren't you?" Manick turned to Shelley.

Shelley did not answer.

"Is it an emergency?" Maya asked.

Shelley wondered what he'd say. There was not much left in his village, Gopala. Only Shelley's father, a high school English teacher. His baba. Aging and balding fast, Baba had decided to spend the rest of his years in the easy chair that he had inherited from his father. There was a family maid in the house to look after him. Shelley's ma and two sisters were in Kolkata, across the border. *Any emergency?* Shelley repeated the question to himself. He was not going to Gopala to see his baba. He was going for Roxana.

"He's going to get married," Manick said.

Shelley frowned at Manick.

"What?" Maya's eyes traveled from her brother to Shelley.

Shelley lowered his eyes as his ears got hot.

"You . . . really?" Her voice changed. Then a smile hung about her half-open mouth.

Whether her smile was a sign of shock or surprise, Shelley could not tell. She congratulated him and walked out of the room just as quickly as she'd walked in. His face tingled for a minute.

A year back—no, more than that—Shelley had met Maya the first time he visited Dream Garden. There was something seductive about her. She had sparkling eyes, and her sharp words lingered with the listener long after the conversation ended.

"Do you write poetry?" she asked.

"Me? Well . . ." Shelley flushed. "Sometimes." He was used to this moment every time he met someone. But he played dumb here. "How do you know?"

"It's in your name. That you're a poet."

"Oh."

"I don't mean the English poet Shelley. I mean that when someone here takes the name 'Shelley,' he definitely writes poetry."

"Ahh," Shelley said. "I get it. No, mine is genuine. Shelley Majumder."

"Shelley Majumder? Your genuine name?"

"My genuine, official name." He handed her his university ID.

Maya looked at the card for five seconds. "Tell me the story of how you got that name."

Shelley started with his grandfather. Although a homeopathic doctor by profession, his grandpa had a good knowledge of Sanskrit. The great Sanskrit poet Kalidasa was his favorite. Therefore, he named his son Kalidasa Majumder. Shelley's father, Kalidasa Majumder, studied English and loved the Romantic poets. Above all, Percy Bysshe Shelley stole his heart. So, Kalidasa Majumder named his son Shelley Majumder.

"So, who is your favorite poet?" Maya asked eventually.

Shelley half laughed. Stole a glimpse of her left cheek. She had a Marilyn Monroe beauty spot.

"What's funny?" She bit her lower lip.

"You actually want to know"—he blinked—"what name will be given to my son, if I have one?"

"Exactly! You're very smart. Not shy like I suspected you were."

"That's the first question I'm asked whenever I tell people how I got my name."

"So, what do you answer them?"

"Yeats. I most admire the Irish poet Yeats."

"Yeats? You'll name your son Yeats?"

"What's wrong with Yeats?"

"Poor kid." She cocked her head.

CHAPTER TWO

1

The house was on about two acres. From the dirt road a path through the canopy of sundry trees led to a pond. Then a narrower path along the bank shaded by khejur and tal palm trees took one to the main residence. The large front yard was visible with a stately neem tree, an unkempt garden, and an abandoned cowshed in the corner. The corrugated-metal-roofed home surrounded by trees had succumbed to the drowsiness of the afternoon heat.

The night train Shelley had taken from Dhaka broke down near Laksam Junction. There was a three-hour delay, and it was almost noon when Shelley arrived in Gopala. His unexpected arrival caught Baba off guard.

"You wrote you were coming next month," Baba said. "Is everything okay?"

Shelley told Baba that he'd gotten a few days off, and he was fine and in perfect health. He handed Baba what he loved most: newspapers. Then, after lunch, he stretched out on his bed and drifted off.

Shelley shook himself awake after a while and caught a smiling face at the window. He narrowed his eyes for a moment. Then smiled back.

Laloo was standing there, his face glued to the wooden window bars. "Waiting for you to wake up."

Laloo—parentless and homeless—looked after cows. "Me know you coming today," he said. "I told her." By "her," Shelley knew he meant Roxana. "She coming in the afternoon."

Shelley checked his watch: 2:44 p.m.

He rolled out of bed. "What did you have for lunch, Laloo?"

"Dal and rice."

"Want to eat something?"

"No. Me not hungry."

"You're never hungry. Why is that?"

Laloo grinned.

—

Next to the river, the cremation ghat was at the far end of the village. It was the last days of summer. Cotton candy kans grass had started to bloom and would soon turn the riverbank into a dreamy white land. Beneath the Kalachand's banyan canopy, at the mouth of the cremation ghat, a red cow was grazing.

"You take care of that cow?" Shelley asked Laloo.

Two nods and a smile. Laloo put his head down, wriggled his big toe in the ground.

A hint. He had something to say. Shelley waited.

With his large button nose and thin lips, Laloo reddened, then said in a near whisper, "My wife, Lali."

"This cow is your wife?"

His goateed chin was glued to his chest. His toenails began to dig into the dirt.

Laloo might have been stupid, but he never lied.

"Well, you do all the stuff with her then? Like a husband and wife do?" Shelley said.

Laloo scratched his head, nodded twice again with a smile.

Shelley looked over at the cow. An ordinary heifer. Large liquid eyes. Glossy red hide. Virgin udders. She looked up at Shelley from the grass. Twitched an ear. Mooed softly.

When Shelley was growing up, the other kids delighted in chasing the stupid boy. They called him "Laloo idiot." They threw stones at him or got on his nerves for fun. Shelley always tried to dissuade them. When he talked to the boy, he found that there were many things he didn't know about that the stupid boy did. Like how female ducks behaved on the water after mating. Or how cows, when in heat, mooed differently.

Once the boy told him he'd tried dog's milk. He hadn't meant to. He was watching the puppies suckling milk from the mummy dog's teats. Eyes closed, she was lying on her side. Abruptly he squatted, leaned forward, made room for himself among the puppies, and put his mouth over a teat and sucked. The bitch raised her head in surprise. She didn't bark, didn't seem to mind. The puppies didn't mind, either. They accepted him as a brother.

Laloo was a late talker. His four-legged friends were okay with that. The company of any animal thrilled him more than humans. Thus, he found his life's purpose: to be with animals. And just like an animal, his five senses flourished. But his tongue would get tangled in his mouth when it came to talking with humans. With those closest to him he could speak, but with the rest he had to make do with nodding and barely talking. In fact, he had little interest in talking. There was nothing like watching a hen walking around with her chicks. Or ducklings swimming with their mother. Or a bitch with a litter of frolicking puppies. Morn to noon and noon to night, he lived in a world of animals, fascinated, obsessed.

Laloo's father died before he was born, and his mother died when he was eight. The village folks soon found out what the orphan boy was good at. They employed him to graze and watch their cows, buffaloes, or goats. They offered him free meals every now and then. What amazed them was that the boy never asked for food of his own. Like the animals he took care of, Laloo understood love. Sometimes, he would go to some house and stand by the kitchen as a silent shadow. Women would bring a plate of rice for him.

No one could tell when Laloo stopped eating meat. Villagers offered him meat on occasion. He would shake his head. *Me no meat! Me no meat!* Every year, during the festival of sacrifice, Laloo disappeared—no one knew where—for a few days.

Laloo, Shelley assumed, would hide in some woods. Deep down in the spinney. He would sit in silence and ask God to turn him into a tree. Like Kalachand's banyan tree. Trees had a grand life. They did not worry about food. Did not fight. Did not kill. Did not kick around animals. But look at humans. Worst of all creatures, they took from trees, animals. In return what did they give? Poop and pee!

2

Roxana turned up in a sky-blue salwar kameez.

"It's on Friday," she reminded Shelley. Her head leaned on his shoulder.

"I know. Five more days." He caressed her fine hair. Her ankle-long tresses were tied up in a big bun behind her head.

Inside the cremation ghat, right and left, unused firewood, heaps of charred wood, and a few broken clay pots lay strewn about. Here everything was strange and silent. Thick with trees and bushes. Over the years, for Shelley and Roxana, it had been a secure location to meet. They were standing by the mango tree they had planted together. It had not yet started to fruit; presumably it would next year.

The sun was dull inside this death-land. So was the air, though no corpse had been cremated recently. Shelley took Roxana in his arms. Her lips spread into a dimpled smile. Four months of separation since his last visit. It was the longest time since he had moved to Dhaka three years earlier.

"Why worry?" He tapped her back. "We know our fate."

Her dark eyes locked with his. "Yes," she said, "we've been planning this for a long time."

"Then cheer up. Tell me about him."

"About whom?" she said, breaking the embrace.

"The man your father arranged for you to marry."

"It's not funny."

"Oh, don't be angry. I'm just curious. What does he do?"

"A banker in Karachi."

"A banker? Seems like a good catch."

Her hand reached for his belly skin.

"Ouch!" he cried. "Stop pinching me."

Her fingers relaxed.

"Okay, listen." His voice was somber. "Day after tomorrow. We catch the evening train."

"Tuesday evening?"

"It's safer," he explained. "First they'll search for you in the neighborhood. Then by the time they find out what's happened, we'll be far away."

"No one has ever done such a thing in this village."

"Are you scared, Roxana?"

"You don't know my father."

"Roxana! We'll be fine."

"Yeah . . . I'm just thinking about the disgrace. Father will kill me if he catches me."

"He won't catch us. We'll never come back, honey."

"We're leaving the village forever?"

"Forever."

Shelley told her how they would make the journey. "All you have to do is come to the banyan tree at six. A hired boat will be waiting by the riverbank to take us near the rail station. Once we get on the boat, we'll be all set."

"What about on the train?" she asked. "What if anyone recognizes me?"

"No one will." Shelley shook his head and touched her shoulders. "I bought a burqa for you. You'll wear it on the train."

"Good idea." Roxana paused. "I should leave now."

She had started growing breasts since she was twelve and could rarely stay out long.

He leaned forward to kiss her.

"Please." She put her finger over his mouth. "I can't bear it now. I go all red, you know."

He did know. She always blushed. Other times he wouldn't have listened, but they were getting married within days. He could save his kisses for later.

"Oh," Roxana said and pulled out something from her waist, near her salwar's drawstring. "This is for you." She shoved it into Shelley's hand.

It was a diary letter. She occasionally wrote long letters and handed them to him when they met.

"I'll see if I can come tomorrow."

Shelley nodded. As he watched Roxana go, he reflected on their early days. Roxana went to Parimal's every other day to fetch fresh paan leaves for her granny. On her way back she often had a brief date with him. Love! Love! He wondered how it had all happened.

She had still been a little girl, ten. He was fifteen. His friends whispered about her. *Roxana*. Beautiful, long-haired, such an innocent face. In a strange kind of way, a bizarre sensation had seized him. He didn't know it was love until some years later when he kissed her. It had been a quiet summer noon. Her cheeks exploded the moment his lips touched hers. His heart pounded, and he shivered all over because right after kissing, he blurted out: *I love you.*

—

On the grass Laloo was lying by the cow, a blade of grass between his milk-white teeth. He often ate grass when he got hungry, only out of habit.

"Hey, you still eat grass?"

Laloo sat up, flashed his teeth. "Chewing feels good."

Shelley plopped himself down before him, plucked a blade of grass, and bit into it. He spat it out.

"Laloo," Shelley said, "Roxana and I are doing something serious this time."

"Se-rious?" he repeated.

"Yeah. But this is all a secret. I'll tell you later." He sighed and lay on the grass.

3

At home, Shelley sat by the window and unfolded Roxana's diary letter, three pages in total.

Father was eating lunch. Mother was serving. And I, following my habit, was standing behind the door—in case Father needed anything, so I could fetch it from the kitchen. Katal fish was the main curry.

"Found a husband for Roxana," Father said, punctuating his words with a distinct chewing sound. "My friend's son. A gentle boy. Works for a bank in Karachi. Karachi . . . a nice city. He will take Roxana with him after the marriage."

Mother listened.

"What do you think?" Father asked. His mouth slurped, sucking the giant katal fish head.

Father asking for Mother's opinion seemed odd to me. I have never heard them talk together. It is always Father who does all the talking. And it is always Mother who does all the listening. Behind the door, not seeing Father's face, I knew the words Mother was going to say. The words that would make her husband happy: Do what you think is best for Roxana.

But Mother spoke unexpected words, with terrible pauses. "Karachi is . . . far . . . maybe a husband from nearby . . ."

Father was still. The next instant his plate dashed against the door I was standing behind. While the plate bounced musically, the rice scattered across the floor, and the katal head, mouth half open and brain half eaten, squirmed, as if it had a last chance to get its life back.

"You stupid woman!" Father roared. "Be a woman. Don't try to step into men's business. I know what will be good for Roxana." He rose and burst out of the room.

The fish had come from the large dighee pond. Every time people fish there, the biggest catch must be sent to Father. Do you remember once you told me that you long to try the biggest catch of the dighee pond? Just one time in your life.

Since then, I don't even touch the curries cooked with the biggest catch. When Mother asks, I say I can't stand the smell of big fish.

You know, often I wonder about Mother. How does she, with her dainty feet, as noiseless as a cat's, crawl into Father's bed every night? Don't his long arms give her a fright? His presence in the house is enough to scare a tiger.

Father drank tiger's milk. You heard that story, right? Let me retell it to you. When Father was little, he suffered from chronic dysentery. Homeopathy, allopathy, ayurveda—nothing worked. Nothing cured him. Then on a snake charmer's advice he was given tiger's milk. It worked: he recovered fully. How did they manage tiger's milk? Well, that winter a circus troupe set up their tent by the river. Their tiger gave birth to two cubs. The circus sardar sold a tiny amount of milk to my grandpa for taka 100.

With tiger's milk in his stomach, Father grew up without a smile on his face. Granny said it was because he was born on a cloudy night in the month of Ashar. But Father grew up healthy, becoming bigger, stronger, and developing a tiger's heart and temper in the flesh of a man.

If only Granny were alive! Perhaps she could have delayed my marriage. Granny was the only one Father listened to, obeyed. But when religion stands between us, I think there is very little even Granny could have done.

4

A newspaper, neatly folded, was on Baba's lap. He must have finished reading every inch of it, even the advertisements. Under the shadow of a neem tree, breathing in the healing breeze, he remained seated in his inherited easy chair. That was what he did all day long during the school holidays. From morning to the last gold light of evening. The only time he dragged himself inside was when it rained. In this same teak easy chair, Baba's father had also spent the best chunk of his life.

From that chair, Baba gave lessons to students who came to him for private tutoring. Up until last winter Roxana had come here for English lessons. She started coming in her fifth grade and had just finished her schooling.

Baba's eyes were staring into the distance. "Baba," Shelley said, "what do you look at here all day?"

"I listen, too," Baba said. His face, scarred with smallpox, beamed from behind his untrimmed beard.

"Listen to what?"

"The music. The silent melody."

Baba folded his left arm under his head. "It's like a theater," he said. "You watch, hear, and enjoy. I hear the birds singing. Watch them bustling in the branches. Watch people pass on the road down there."

"You like it?" Shelley said.

"Yes. But I don't understand."

"Understand what?"

Baba's eyes turned vague, vacant. "I was little once. Grew big. Got married. Had children. Got pretty much what I wanted. I've seen India fall apart. Seen Pakistan." His face slowly rolled over to face Shelley. "But I often wonder. What's the point?"

The nebulous thinking of Baba's aging brain baffled Shelley. Did he mean the Partition? Or the point of life itself? Or was it some unresolved theory about his own life? Baba knew pre-partitioned Kolkata like a book. But he had never been to Dhaka. He had never needed to, anyway.

When Pakistan was still India, Baba had been a BA student at the University of Calcutta. Shelley's grandpa had had so many mouths to feed, and he advised his son in a letter to study at his own expense. Baba did that for three months. Then one morning he was back in Gopala, without informing his father, without finishing his degree.

Shelley peered at Baba's moving lips, but the voice was muffled.

"Everything falls apart," the old lips muttered, as if to himself. His face a little flustered.

Shelley fumbled for words to reply to Baba. He shrank from his father's sullen gaze, as if it were all his fault. The breaking up of India was all his fault. All his fault that West Bengal and East Bengal—one culture, one language—were no longer one country. His fault that his mother and sisters no longer lived with them in the same country.

It had been over three years since his ma and sisters left for India. When the 1964 riots broke out, Ma became frightened. Terror-struck, she spent sleepless nights chanting deliriously to Baba, "This country is not safe for Hindus. We should've left right after the Partition. Think about our young daughters . . ."

That year in July, Baba made the arrangements, but excluded himself. Ma begged, but Baba was firm: "I was born on this soil. This is my country." He spelled out his fear, too. He had a respectable job here. What would he do after relocating to India? Rot away like a refugee?

Shelley had stayed with Baba.

"I think," Baba said after a long pause, "I will die like my father. Sleeping peacefully in this easy chair."

A cold silence, under the shadow of the neem foliage, crept in. Out of Shelley's heart came a heavy exhale.

"Are you getting lonely, Baba? You want to see Ma?"

Baba didn't answer. His glance lingered over the pond, unchanged. But the spirit inside the aging body inside the everyday kurta-pajamas seemed to be elsewhere. Maybe elsewhere catching up with the past.

5

Beneath the big banyan tree, Laloo was sound asleep. Above him a medium-sized brown cobra lay nestled on a distant branch. They both looked calm, dead to the world in the afternoon light. A lonely owl, sitting on a top branch, moved its head now and then. A deep slumber in this eerie place was possible for none but Laloo and the animals.

The banyan tree, according to Gopala lore, was a man named Kalachand, whose veins grew into roots and covered mile after mile of Gopalan area. There was a time when the river would lend things on occasion to the villagers. Gold vessels and utensils would surface from beneath the river as and when requested. Once they had used them, people returned them. Until eventually a wicked woman in the village did not return a golden spoon. Nothing had emerged from the river since.

Shelley sat down. The slumbering Laloo, half naked, was sleeping like a child. Suntanned from head to toe. Dusty, bare feet. His lungi caked with mud, the ends tucked in at the waist, covering his crotch. A bamboo stick, his constant companion, lying beside him. His tallish, skinny body reeked of the dung and urine of cows.

Close by, grazing, were two cows. Shelley recognized the red cow. Lali, the wife of Laloo. The very instant Lali looked up at Shelley, she started urinating. *Chit chit chit.*

Shelley laughed to himself. When they were little, he and Laloo had real pissing contests. They stood inches apart and urinated together to see who could hit the farthest point.

It was getting late. No sign of Roxana, he thought. Had she left any message in the secret place? Would she be able to leave tomorrow, safe and sound? Would she?

Shelley roused Laloo. He sat up with a start, rubbed his eyes, smiled.

Shelley pointed to the branch where the cobra was still resting.

Laloo peered up. Squinted. Yawned.

"It's not funny," Shelley said.

"They don't bite. You do nothing, they do nothing."

Shelley observed him admiringly. Then: "Hey, you heard anything? Roxana hasn't showed up."

"Oh," he gushed, remembering something. From his lungi waist he handed Shelley a piece of paper. "Roxana told me to come here with this. Me came and fell asleep."

The crumpled paper was damp from perspiration, but still readable.

"You're having your weekly meal at Roxana's house this evening?" Shelley asked him, reading the note.

He nodded.

"I'll give you a note to pass to her."

After a moment, Laloo looked around. "Me have a secret to tell you." His voice almost a whisper.

Shelley stared at him.

"Me growing a horn on my head." He scratched his crown.

Shelley pulled on Laloo's long sunburnt hair to examine his head. On top of his scalp he saw a tiny round spot that felt hard and bony. Swollen and thick, the patch grew a pointed protrusion.

"It could be something else," Shelley told him.

"No." Laloo shook his head. "Me had a dream."

Shelley said nothing.

"Me know me not got brains in my head. They say it's all cow dung."

Shelley listened. Laloo was the happiest person he knew. Laloo could count up to five and never took on responsibility for more than five cows. He loved what he did—milking, cleaning, and grazing the cows. To the villagers he was as useful as a cow: cheap, hardworking, long-suffering, unresisting. At night he slept comfortably in grocery wholesaler Chowdhury's cowshed, along with three cows, on scanty straw. As compensation for taking care of Chowdhury's cows, Laloo received two meals every day.

6

Shelley pushed the half-open door. It parted with a long creaking. A house gecko scurried across the earthen floor.

Shelley stood in the middle of the room. The window facing the mango grove was ajar, a sliver of sun slipping through it. The dingy room still smelled of homeopathic medicine. Once it had been Grandpa's study. Grandpa spent most of his time inside these four walls. Ten years on since his death, stagnant dust and a sweet-smelling medicinal air pervaded every corner of the place. Grandpa's picture on the tin wall had faded, the blurred edges looking like dried bay leaf. In that photo he wore a kurta-pajama made of khadi clothes and a Gandhi topi cap. All white. In the 1930s he had abandoned his European clothes and followed Gandhi's khadi movement. Until his last day he wore clothes made of only handspun khadi. Shelley was eleven when he died.

Behind thin glass doors a wooden bookshelf contained his old tomes and corked medicine bottles. Shelley stared at the top of the cupboard. There sat Grandpa's shoes, thick with dust and tangled cobwebs. Thirty-five years ago, the shoes had been raven black. At the time, Grandpa practiced homeopathy in Kolkata. One day he took a tram ride wearing his shiny shoes, and sitting across from him was a white man who stepped on his shoe twice on purpose. *What is wrong with you?* Grandpa asked. But the white man looked the other way and giggled. As the tram reached the next stop, Grandpa trod on the white man's shoe hard, yelled in his face, "You jackass," and jumped out of the carriage. Shelley grew up hearing this story an infinite number of times.

Toward the end of his life, Grandpa suffered from chronic constipation. All his life he had always had his bowel movement in the morning. If delayed, it made his day worse, as if the sun hadn't come up. During his last days this occurred regularly, up to three or four days a week. Sometimes even all week. Shelley could picture Grandpa half lying in the easy chair, his worrying face denoting a delayed bowel action. Whoever greeted him, he would mention that he'd had a bad start to the day: "Been to toilet five times already, nothing happened."

Shelley waded through the frozen air of the room and opened the window wide to look outside. The solitary mango grove resembled the home of an orphaned boy. Somewhere in there a pair of sparrows was conversing; a pigeon cooed. Yet the corpselike trees seemed unusually quiet. A gentle breeze from the grove opened a past chapter of Shelley's life.

When he and his two sisters were small, the mango grove buzzed with their shouts and screams. During mango season if there was the sound of falling fruit in the evening, Shelley would spar with his elder sister.

"It's Langra mango," he would say.

"No. Fazli."

"It can't be. Don't you know the sound?"

And the squabble would go on and on until their parents shouted at them to shut up. Then they spoke in whispered words, declaring that one would wake up before the other and collect all the ripe mangoes. The moment they woke the next morning, they dashed for the grove to collect the fallen fruit. Their little sister always had them promise, before closing her eyes, to wake her up at dawn for mango collection.

Shelley sighed. His ma and two sisters were now in another country, in another part of Bengal. He half shut the window and stepped out of the room.

The day was aglow in the yard, the morning sun turning hot. Shelley found Baba sunbathing in the easy chair, with a book in his hands. He was rereading *A Passage to India*. A thought struck Shelley. Maybe he would have the same fate as Baba. With an unfinished degree, he might end up in that hereditary easy chair. Where once his grandpa lived and died.

7

Under the sun Shelley sat on a stool rubbing mustard oil on his body. When his skin had sucked up enough oil, he descended into the pond. The water welcomed him, cooled him off. He felt every movement of his limbs. His body swayed like a pendulum in the water. He stretched, swam slowly. Baba, from his easy chair under the neem tree, watched his son swimming.

Shelley stood waist-deep in the water and soaped his upper body. He thought of the last evening in Dream Garden. To his wonderment, he saw Marilyn Monroe's face swaying on the water. No, not Marilyn. It was Maya—Maya Monroe.

Once, during a power outage, he and Maya had been alone in the living room. "Let me get a candle," Maya said, picking her way to the kitchen, leaving him in the dark. Back she came, cradling a candle in one hand and covering the flickering flame with the other so the wind could not blow it out. And the candle created a halo around her face, as if she were the moon, dazzling.

—

Over lunch, crunching crispy ilish fish tail, Shelley pondered: Should he tell Baba that he was leaving in the afternoon?

"Can you manage with the money you earn there?" Baba asked.

"You mean the movie magazine? Yes."

"Don't overwork. If you need money, let me know."

"The job is easy. I have no office hours. I go whenever I want."

Then Baba brought up politics. "Anti-Ayub protests are soaring in Dhaka."

"Not only in Dhaka. Everywhere across East Pakistan. Student organizations are getting proactive."

"Do you attend rallies and protests?"

"Often."

Baba looked at his face. Be careful not to get distracted from your studies, he seemed to say.

—

I am following my heart. You have always taught me to do that.

Shelley wrote the note for Baba. He thought a minute, and then added a quote from John Keats.

I am certain of nothing but the holiness of the heart's affections.

Baba hated inventing lies out of fear. "Fear and love cannot coexist," Baba said frequently. "If you don't love me, I'm okay with that. But I don't want my children to fear me."

It was not about fear. It was better sometimes, Shelley reasoned, not to explain everything. Besides, Baba would be constantly perturbed, finding no solution for the problem: a marriage between a Hindu and a Muslim was impossible on the soil of this village. Baba would not mind, but Roxana's father definitely would. For more than a dozen years her father had been the head of Gopala village. Shelley knew he would rather kill his daughter than allow this shame to occur.

On one level it was very positive, Shelley reflected, that Ma and his sisters were not here. His elopement would have upset them. The future of his sisters would have been at risk.

Shelley left the note on Baba's bedroom desk. A family picture was hanging over the desk on the tarnished tin wall. Ma, Baba, Grandpa at the back, and in front of them nine-year-old Shelley and his two sisters. Shelley let out a sigh. Old photographs had an odor of melancholy that saddened, suffocated the heart. You couldn't keep staring at them for too long. He slipped out of the room.

The ancient maid was asleep in the spare room, dead to the world. She wouldn't notice anything. Shelley had always reckoned she was born old, for he had always seen her the same. Grey and wrinkled. Old and stooped.

Shelley picked up his small bag and padded out of the rear of the house.

Along the road he paused and looked back at the path that led to the house, where he had been born. This was the path his mother and grandmother had walked to enter the house for the first time. This was the path his father and grandfather had walked to go to Kolkata. This was the path he had walked to and from school. This was the path that had carried Grandpa to the cremation ghat.

He sighed and slunk away.

At the riverbank a pansi boat was waiting. Roxana would be here at six o'clock. From Gopala, an hour by boat. Then a mile on foot to the railway station. The Dhaka Mail departed at nine.

8

Shelley waited and worried. He paced up and down the bush-clad riverbank by the cremation ghat. He rubbed his chin and peered in the distance for the slightest sign. Nothing there. The Timex on his wrist ticked on. It was nearly seven o'clock. The sun had already set, and it would be dark soon. He broke into a sweat. If Roxana didn't show up in another twenty minutes, they would miss the train.

At last a woman's figure emerged in the distance. The woman strode past the jute field, past the tal palm tree and kans grassland, and neared the cremation ghat. Shelley exhaled in a rush of hot air.

Roxana arrived at the water's edge.

The pansi boat had a curtained bamboo canopy for shade. Shelley drew the curtains at both ends. As they settled into the deck, the boat headed off. He touched Roxana's hand. It was cold.

"What happened? You're late."

"I'm sorry. A guest came." Her gaze was still on the water, unchanged.

On the water the golden skies glistened. Through the swaying curtain she peered at the bank. Shelley followed her eyes. He could see what they were leaving behind. Their childhood. Their families. The good times. The bad times. The image of an easy chair bobbed up out of the gilded waters. And a lonely face, solemn and serene, in repose. Shelley drew a long breath and let it out.

"Here's your burqa." He handed Roxana a paper bag.

She glanced at the bag but did not open it.

The boat entered the main river.

CHAPTER THREE

1

Fulbaria Station, Dhaka. The train came to its final stop and hissed profusely. At once all the dormant souls of the train awoke from a quiescent mood. Soon the loud murmur of passengers blended with the platform pandemonium. Everyone was in a hurry, frantic to disembark the train. Some were climbing out through the windows as fish jump out of a fishing net. People were pushing, hustling, bustling, and moving madly in the direction of the departure gate.

Shelley waited until the carriage cleared out. Roxana, behind her black burqa, busied herself eying the packed platform through the window. It was her first time in Dhaka. She looked overwhelmed. The hullabaloo, she told him, reminded her of the village market day. But way more crowded. More cries and noises.

"Let's go." He touched her back. He climbed down from the carriage. Roxana stood at the door and unveiled her face for the first time since they started the journey. As Shelley helped her out of the carriage, the sun kissed her cheeks.

The crowd on the platform grew thin. Outside the railway station, the clamor of passengers, porters, hawkers, horse carriages, rickshaws—all created a fine chorus. Roxana stuck to Shelley closely, clutching his hand, the way a little daughter clutched her father's hand at a funfair. He hired a rickshaw for a downtown restaurant.

"O mago! So many people!" she said in the rickshaw. Her grip released his arm.

"That's what a city is like."

"It's scary!"

He laughed and put his hand around her back. "Nothing to be scared of, I'm with you."

As the rickshaw rolled forward, Roxana took a breath. The morning air felt fresh here. She looked in his eyes and smiled. "I can't believe I'm in Dhaka. With you!"

"Yes. It's us. You and me."

"I still can't believe." A pause. Then, "Wow!"

"What?"

"The building. Oh my, it has a big clock!"

"That's the DIT building. Tallest building in Dhaka."

Roxana didn't move her eyes form the DIT tower clock until another building blocked her sight.

The ride to the restaurant was brief. Shelley took a private table, ordered naan bread, mixed vegetable, and milk tea at the end. Roxana ate a little. When the steaming milk tea arrived, she stared at the cups. The cups were brimming with tiny bubbles that threatened to overflow. Bits of milk skin swam in the tea. She took a sip and said, "Tastes delicious."

"I often come here only for the tea." He looked over at her. "Are you okay?"

"As long as you're with me," she said, shifting her eyes from a waiter serving the corner table, "I'm fine wherever we are."

—

The mouth of the alley, as always, was littered with garbage, reeking of an overpowering foul smell. Roxana squeezed her face and covered her nose. Shelley was used to the stench. He paid the fare and ushered Roxana down the narrow lane. At the end of the alleyway, Shelley ceased before his mossy, old brick wall house.

"Here we are." He unlocked the padlock of the main gate.

They entered.

Roxana took a good look around her, standing in the small yard.

This moss-blanketed house at the end of the alleyway was a good bargain. He'd been here roughly six months. Without electricity and running water, but with a tiny yard, the house gave him the flavor of village life. And this simple privacy, albeit dark and damp, and plaster flaking off the walls in places exposing the naked bricks, fascinated him more than the communal life of the university hall of residence where he'd been earlier.

Shelley unlocked the room's door. The door opened with a creak. Once the two large windows were open, the room woke up from its dullness.

A double bed, a clothes stand, a desk overflowing with books—this was the room.

He put a hand around her waist while she strolled around.

"I like the yard," she announced.

"The rent is cheap. Because there's no electricity, no running water."

"No water?"

"I have a maid who fills that matka every other day." He showed her the round earthen matka jar he kept outside. "If the landlord renovates this building, the rent will be doubled."

The landlord had reasons not to give the house a makeover, he mentioned. The rumor was that the owner had grabbed this land from a Hindu family who had left for India after the Partition. Now the property was still under litigation.

"I'm a village girl. Never used electricity. I'll be fine here as it is."

"It's not that bad, in fact. You get lots of light and air."

Roxana stood at the door, gazing across the yard at the hibiscus plant.

"Are you okay?" Shelley asked again, stroking her shoulder.

"Mhmm," she said.

Between his hands Shelley cradled her face. His eyes zoomed in on her mouth. Her lips were heart shaped. Her groove right beneath her nose was geometric, beautifully curved. That tiny wonder tantalized him like a puzzle. He brushed dewy sweat off her top lip. Her mouth grabbed his grazing finger. A gentle bite held his finger between her teeth.

"You have lovable lips," he said.

Roxana smiled and nestled her head against his chest. A few seconds. Then she broke away. "Oho, I forgot. We're not married yet."

"I see. Very well. We can head to the kazi's whenever you're ready."

"I'll have a quick wash, and then I'm all set."

2

The marriage registrar office was a small corrugated iron structure with a large veranda at the front. The door was wide open. Inside, a decrepit old table. Five shabby chairs kept it company. Two wooden frames hung on the wall: Allahu calligraphy in the right frame, an image of Kaaba Sharif in the left.

It turned out the kazi lived inside and used the veranda as his office. Shelley gave a small cough, to announce their presence.

In response a face peeped out. The man was clearly in pajamas and an undershirt.

Two minutes later the kazi appeared dressed up. His face, bearded and dyed with henna, was broad. He wore a knitted skullcap. But his eyes fazed Shelley. They were shifty and looked strangely at Roxana.

The kazi was chewing paan leaves. He motioned Shelley to the front chairs to sit. "Want to wed?" His jaw moved nosily as he spoke. But his eyes were still on Roxana.

Shelley nodded, and in that instant realized the kazi was cross-eyed.

The kazi pulled out a chair at his side, settled down, and ran his fingers through his henna-dyed beard.

Roxana stood behind Shelley. He glanced at her, and they both sat down.

The kazi started probing. It was more like an interview. Shelley answered, evading direct eye contact with the kazi. He told him there was love between himself and Roxana, but their marriage was opposed on religious grounds. He now wanted to convert to Islam in order to marry her.

The kazi leaned back in his chair. "You have two witnesses?" he inquired.

Shelley did not understand.

The kazi explained. According to Islam, two males were required as witnesses to perform a marriage.

For this Shelley was unprepared. He asked the kazi if he could find them some witnesses. The kazi licked his lips, now reddened with paan juice. His cross-eyes flicked between Roxana and Shelley. Then he stood up, told them to wait, and went out.

A civil marriage was another option and would not require Shelley's conversion to Islam. Initially he had preferred this idea, but that British-made law required the bride to be at least eighteen years old, and Roxana was sixteen. Therefore that option was not available to them.

The kazi returned with two older men. Their clothing suggested he had found them at a nearby mosque. The two men sat next to Shelley.

Becoming a Muslim was much easier than Shelley had thought. It all came down to saying a simple phrase: La ilaha illallah, Muhammadur rasul-ullah. *There is no true God but Allah, and Muhammad is the Messenger of Allah.* Saying this, one became a Muslim.

Thus Shelley became a Muslim.

Following the conversion, the kazi insisted that he take a new name, a Muslim name. Shelley refused. With his little knowledge about Islam, he pointed out that this was not obligatory. What really did matter was belief, not names. Moreover, his last name, Majumder, was common both in Hindu and Muslim households. The kazi yielded.

When all the due process and paperwork were over, the kazi coughed, cleared his throat. "This is embarrassing," he began. "Actually, I don't know how to put it, but I feel it's my Islamic duty to inform you. Actually, you know . . . a Muslim man must be circumcised."

For this Shelley was also unprepared. His eyes flickered under the kazi's gaze. As if the piercing gaze were inspecting his lingam between his legs. His shoulders hunched and unhunched. Partition again, he thought. That male organ was the main point of the Partition. India had been partitioned on the grounds of circumcision. That was the issue Jinnah, Nehru, Gandhi had fought for. And thus the two nations were born. One circumcised. Another uncircumcised.

"Not to worry," the Kazi said. "Actually, for this type of case, I've a special arrangement. Just a few days of bed rest. Not a big deal. You've become a Muslim. You ought to do it as early as possible."

Roxana sneezed, almost inaudibly.

"Yes, yes. I am aware of that," Shelley replied fast. He wished Roxana were not there. He interlocked his fingers. Rubbed the right thumb across the left thumb, and the left across the right. Harder and harder.

"You're an educated man. Actually, you know, circumcision has lots of benefits. Science has proven it's good for a healthy sexual life—"

"Yes, yes. I know all that." His face tightened. Jumping to his feet, Shelley drew the wallet from his pocket. He paid the kazi's fees and left a tip as well. Then he strode off with Roxana.

3

From New Market Roxana bought, at Shelley's insistence, two saris and three sets of salwar kameez. Out on the main road in the soft afternoon light, they were about to climb on a horse-drawn carriage when somebody called out, "Shelley sir!"

Shelley looked over his shoulder. "Hey, King Siraj!" he said.

King Siraj flashed a big smile. His face was sweaty. A grubby shirt hung loosely over the boy's greasy shorts. He was barefoot.

Shelley introduced him to Roxana. "This street boy is the youngest political activist in Dhaka. If it's a protest or a mass meeting or a demo— he's there. He's everywhere. Doesn't matter if he goes hungry, you will always hear his voice chanting the slogans."

King Siraj looked at Roxana quizzically. "Y-your wife, sir?"

Shelley nodded.

"Hoo. She is b-b-beautiful!"

Roxana smiled.

"So, what's the latest?" Shelley asked.

"Six-point movement, sir. A big protest tomorrow. You coming?"

"I'm busy."

The boy gave his cheeky adult grin. The grin that meant, *I know why*.

"Okay." Shelley raised his hand to wave goodbye. "See you, little comrade."

The horses started to move, and the carriage rolled away.

"How old is that politics boy?" Roxana said.

"King Siraj? Ten or eleven, I guess."

"Quite mature for his age. Is 'King' his real name?"

"No way. We call him that."

"Why does he call you 'sir'?"

"He calls all the university people 'sir.' He spends most of his time around the Dhaka University campus. The students like him. He doesn't have to worry about going hungry." Shelley described how King Siraj occasionally walked over to a policeman with nimble steps and broke wind noisily. "He calls it a fart-bomb. He says police faces make him fart."

"Farting at the police?" She laughed. "That's worse than mooning."

Halfway down the road Shelley said, "It's not safe to head home now."

Roxana regarded him steadily.

Her father might hunt them down here, he explained. To stay safe and sound, it'd be wise to be away from his home for a few days.

Roxana clutched his hand. She couldn't believe her father's ferocious grip could reach them in Dhaka.

Shelley told the driver to drive toward Tanti Bazaar. Along the way, he bought some sweets.

"Listen," Shelley said to her, "we'll be staying at my friend Krishna's. But he's not there. He and all his family moved to India. Only a widowed auntie lives there by herself. She knows about you. I told her once."

"She lives all alone?"

"Well, I presume they left her to protect the house from being squatted in."

The building was at a dead end. Shelley led Roxana through a dim, damp staircase to the upper floor. The musty air smelled depressing. On the wooden door he knocked with his knuckles. The person who opened the door looked more depressing than the house. Shelley couldn't recognize that wrinkled old face of the woman, but he recognized the woman standing behind her.

"Shelley!" Pisi cried in her warm and loud voice. "Where've you been lost?" Pisi walked past the maid and grasped his arm. Then she noticed Roxana. She stood for a second, staring, and let out another cry. "You got married?"

Shelley nodded with a smile. Pisi took Roxana's hand and pulled her into the room. "She's smashing!" She began to scrutinize Roxana from head to toe. Her ankle-length hair impressed Pisi more than anything.

Pisi forgot to tell them to sit. She demanded to know everything all at once. Shelley gave her a brief history.

The maid brought some snacks with the tea. Pisi yelled at her three times to get some water.

"See who I am living with." Pisi looked at Shelley. "A deaf old bag. If I say right, she goes left. For a windbag like me, God's matched a good listener, you see."

Shelley laughed. Roxana giggled.

"Laughing, eh? You didn't even come to see me after they left. Seven months gone. I could have been dead."

Shelley apologized, talked about the recent letter he'd received from Krishna. After a long wait Krishna had taken over a bookstore in College Street, Kolkata.

"Why didn't you go with them, may I ask?" he said.

"Why should I? The small flat there has no space for me. What's the use of an old widow, huh?" Her voice shook as she talked. "I'm good in Pakistan. Queen of this house. The downstairs rent is fine for me to survive on."

The silent sipping of teas went on. The tatty, unkempt cane sofa cracked. Shelley tried to switch the topic. He asked Pisi whether he could spend a few days here with his wife to avoid any risks.

Pisi said sure and asked the deaf maid, at the top of her lungs, to prepare a room quickly. When the room was ready, Pisi drew close to him and lowered her voice.

"Have you slept with the girl yet? Don't be shy."

He knew Pisi wouldn't let it drop. "No," he replied.

"Fantastic. You, child, get some sleep in this room. I'll keep her in my room for the bridal night."

Shelley took a bath. Roxana didn't. A late bath would mean wet hair all night. They fell asleep in different rooms. When he woke up, it was already night and dinner was served. The table was choked with special dishes. Pisi looked every inch excited. He knew that for her, the most painful thing in the world was having dinner alone. It was a long, lingering dinner.

4

In the bedroom Roxana pointed at a discolored wooden frame on the wall, in which a black-and-white photo showed a young man standing and smiling. Behind him were boundless skies and mountains.

"That's Krishna's father," Shelley said.

"Your friend's father?"

"Hmm. I never met his father, only heard of him. He was killed in the riots. He had a jewelry shop nearby that was looted and burned."

"How horrible!" She leaned her head on his chest.

Shelley stroked her back and embraced her. She smelled of jasmine.

"You look magnificent," he said.

Roxana said nothing.

"Are you okay?"

"Feeling bad and sad. Don't know why."

He broke the embrace and said, "I love you."

"I love you, too." Roxana pressed her lips to his.

He had waited for this day. They both had waited. To explore each other in a prime time, in a perfect place, in a pleasurable way. Not like a thief on the cremation ground.

In bed, she asked him to turn off the light. He insisted on keeping it on.

"Don't be greedy. This is the first time I'm undressing before a man." He obeyed.

Roxana began to undo her vermilion wedding sari. Through the window the moon peeped in. In its dim light, her tender hands folded the silk sari with care, and it slid away. Now she was in a short, snug blouse and a petticoat. Shelley approached her.

His hands cupped her face. His trembling fingertips stroked her eyebrows. Her eyelids. Her nose. Her groove. Her lips. Her cheeks. Her chin. His hands grazed her naked neck. Then fell on her blouse, which he started to unbutton. She helped him take it off. No bra inside. Never had she any. He cupped her breasts. Her light-chocolate nipples grew puffy and hard. The tip of his tongue touched them. She shivered. He dove down. Dipped his tongue into the dent of her belly button. Before his saliva soaked her belly button, she restrained him.

"Ooh, it tickles," she moaned.

He attempted to pull her petticoat down. She gripped his hand. He slid the other hand under her petticoat. This time she placed her hand hard over her groin. Underneath, slower than a snail, his hand succeeded in touching her feminine parts. It was wonderfully warm, unshaven, soft like the fresh grasses of the monsoon. He made one more determined attempt to undress her. She still resisted and looked up at him.

"You didn't take off yours," Roxana said.

Shelley removed his clothes and lay in bed. Roxana beamed at him and half lay on his chest. She raised her leg, rested it over his thighs, over his arousal. She slid her hand down there and held him. She said she wondered how it worked, appearing and disappearing.

The first attempt at penetration was unsuccessful. They had another feverish try. And then another. Each time, with a lingering pain, went unrewarded.

"It hurts," she winced.

He had to break the rhythm and returned to bed unsatisfied from the unopening door of her yoni.

5

On Friday morning their day out started with visiting the zoo. Then, after lunch Shelley wanted to give Roxana a glimpse of Central Dhaka. Motijheel Commercial Area would be a good start, he thought. On foot and in a rickshaw, they made their way through the office streets. She gazed at the big buildings, lifting her head up.

At New Market, the problem arose when Roxana turned down the idea of shopping for her underclothes. The sales staff were all male. How could she ask them to show her some undergarments when she was unsure about her own cup size? Also, to determine her size, how could she allow the male eyes to go up and down, looking at her? Not on this planet could she bear the humiliation.

Shelley came up with an idea. He told her to hang around outside while he went inside to buy her intimate apparel.

He went into a small womenswear shop. As he put into words what he wanted, he began to sweat. The salesman asked him about the size. He was in his late teens. That made Shelley more uncomfortable. Finally the salesman showed him different colors of average sizes. Shelley wasted no time, took one average size, one smaller than that, and another bigger than that. In three different colors—skin, red, and black.

With a bag full of mythical excitement, Shelley turned back to Roxana. The complexion of her waiting face, he noticed, matched the pleasant afternoon at New Market.

"We're going to a movie now," he announced to Roxana, checking the time.

—

The movie, *Chakori*, had a romantic story line. Starring Shabana and Nadeem, it set box office records and was extremely popular for its songs. In the cinema, the minute the movie started, Shelley saw Roxana forget this world. Every scene, every shot, everything and anything in the movie moved her. From time to time Shelley placed the flat of his hand on the back of hers.

She came back to the world with a start when in the movie the heroine set out to take her life. During the film's climax, Roxana gripped his arm.

"Let's go home. I'm feeling sick."

"What do you mean?"

"It's urgent," she urged.

On the rickshaw she whispered in his ear, "My period's started."

It was too early, she said. She was unprepared for this untimely menstruation. Nothing embarrassing happened on the ride home, but it couldn't wait until the movie was finished. That disgusted her.

"I'm sorry," she said that night, for now there would be no lovemaking.

"There, there," he said. "We've got the rest of our lives to make enough love."

She still looked glum.

"It's rather good, you know. Consider it serendipity. We can consummate the marriage in our own home."

"I have a question," she said with a tight-lipped smile. It struck her how Draupadi of the Mahabharata managed five husbands. "If one brother has to wait four days to get her back, this wait time naturally lingered during her menstruation, right?"

Shelley laughed. One night with one husband was the policy, he said, but they could sleep together in the daytime as well. "The policy was if one brother was engaged with her, the others wouldn't enter the room."

"Isn't it weird? Being the wife of five men?"

Still, polyandry was a pretty common practice in some places of the Indian subcontinent, he pointed out. And other parts in the world, too. The great benefit of this type of marriage was that land could be kept undivided.

"I want to read a full version of Mahabharata," she said.

"I'll buy you one."

—

The next day after visiting the museum, they had lots of walks, lots of sightseeing, and lots of street food. From the clock tower to Dhaka Stadium, Mir Jumla cannon to Gulistan Cinema, even the evening streetlights were a wonder to Roxana. Yet her imaginary magnificent Dhaka and the real material Dhaka turned out to be dissimilar.

"I thought Dhaka was full of rich people," Roxana said. "But this city appears poorer than our Gopala." Her sharp eyes hadn't missed the stray homeless people living by the railway line. And the half-naked beggars in the streets.

"The light cannot survive without darkness. The rich need the poor to get richer. However, the poverty you see in East Pakistan comes from West Pakistan."

"Oh, I don't get your politics."

"Let me explain to you very simply. Our jute, the golden fiber of Bengal, is famous. We're the largest exporter of jute in the world. More than 50 percent of Pakistan's foreign earnings come from this jute alone. From East Pakistan. Where does this money go? To West Pakistan. They are developing Karachi and Lahore like New York and London with our hard-earned currency. Their spending on education, health care, and other facilities rose twofold, threefold in the West Wing since 1947. And ours? Almost none. But this is our money." Shelley's fist clenched as he spoke. "Our population is larger than the West Wing, but they overlook us. They happily forget that we're bearing their expenses."

"It's just wrong. A clear disparity," Roxana said. Her voice sounded hurt.

"See, you understand politics." He paused. "Accha, how do you like Dhaka?"

"Dhaka? Honestly?"

"Sure."

"Too many people in too little space. Building after building. No green. It's depressing. You cannot walk barefoot on muddy roads or soft grass like in Gopala. No pond to take a nice bath and swim in." She sighed. "It's okay to live here for a while. But it cannot be your home forever."

Shelley took her hand in his. "I feel the same way, Roxana. I miss Gopala, always." After a moment's silence, he said, "The city is a place where everyone is a migrant. We're all stuck here."

—

Back home over dinner, Pisi dropped a bomb.

"Holy cow! You kids are having fun a-all day and a-all night. I'm jealous. Shelley, do me a favor. Find someone for me. I want to have fun like you guys."

Shelley exchanged a glance with Roxana. Her cheeks turned red, and that redness spread to her ears.

"Are you serious?" He turned to Pisi.

"Of course not." Pisi slapped her forehead with her palm. "Holy cow! I'm too old to date. How dare you think like this!" Then she half fell on the floor, laughing.

Later in the bedroom, Roxana offered Shelley two options. Either he turned off the light while she got changed, or she would change in the bathroom.

"I need some time to get used to you, darling!" she said.

Shelley turned the light off.

Roxana swung her back to him to put on her nightwear. In the dark his eyes could sense the rhythm of her anatomy. The darkness was not dark enough to cover her nakedness.

Turning the light back on, Roxana came to bed with a comb in hand. Shelley said to her, "We'll leave for our house tomorrow."

6

Shelley unlocked the Aligarh padlock of his room's door, and a stuffy smell welcomed them. Roxana let her eyes roll around the room, and she sniffed.

"It needs a super sweep," she said.

"I guess so."

She took the broom in her hand. "Is this the only broom you have?"

The broom was near unusable. "I can get you a new one," he said. "I can go right now."

"Do me a favor. Get me pen and paper first."

She checked what he had and had not. What she needed to cook for two. She made a list:

Right away: a broom, a wok, a flat pan, three vessels, utensils
Soon: bedspread, curtains, jug, plates, tumblers

On his way back from Kaptan Bazaar, carrying groceries, Shelley bought biryani for lunch. When he entered the room, Roxana had showered already. Her long black hair was damp, droplets glistening at the ends like dew on grass in the morning. A fresh fragrance of soap emanating from her body and hair filled the room. He buried his nose in her hair.

"You smell so good."

"I just used your soap."

He shrugged and handed her the packets. "Biriyani for lunch."

"Why? I can cook biryani," Roxana said. "We mustn't waste money on restaurant food."

"Okay, okay, I get it."

After the late lunch, Shelley made tea on the kerosene wick stove. On the floor by the door, he spread out newspapers for them to sit on. He lit a cigarette. Roxana tried his Capstan. She took a big gulp, filled her mouth, and then released the smoke.

"Rubbish." She returned the cigarette, wrinkling her nose with her upper lip slightly drawn up.

He took the cigarette between his fingers and thought about tomorrow. Tomorrow was Monday. He had the usual week ahead after having spent an unusual week off. University, work, private tutoring, and then finally home in the evening. That was the real romantic life. Would Roxana be able to cope? All day by herself in this city?

"Oh," said Shelley, "we can visit Manick's tomorrow evening."

"Your university friend?"

"Yes. He's majoring in philosophy. They're Calcatian."

"Calcatian?"

"From Kolkata."

"Wow! I've never met anyone from Kolkata." Roxana planted her head on her knees.

"You can now. With his sister and mother as well."

"Aha. He has a sister."

They had another round of tea. Quietly the sun set. Dusk fell.

"Have you ever noticed," Roxana said, "that there's a strange feeling that takes over us at this hour of the day?"

Shelley stared at her.

"A feeling of blankness. Something that makes you sad for no reason."

"So many evenings I've thought about it, too. Yeah, a strange sadness. When everything seems pointless." He touched her and added, "Tagore captured this melancholy, a similar moment, in one of his beautiful poems. Do you want to hear it?"

She nodded.

He recited in Bengali:

Emon dine tare bola jay
Emon ghanoghor borisay . . .

They were not hungry. Roxana offered to cook something for dinner, but Shelley suggested they have a light snack. Muri makha. Puffed rice with onion, green chili, and mustard oil.

He lit the hurricane lamp. Roxana sat on the floor to chop onions, spreading her hair out on her back. He tried to imagine her ten years from now. A perfect wife with years of experience. With two kids playing around. Busy cooking and looking after the children. Gotten plump. Shelley screeched to a halt in his head. Maybe she should go to college, he thought, rather than become one of those housewives. They would read poetry together. Watch English movies. Discuss politics. Taking a deep breath, he slumped his shoulders. For everything, he needed money. A better job.

Roxana put the plate of muri makha on the bed. They sat across from one another. Just then, Shelley remembered that he had a *Mayfair* magazine and an adult photo chapbook under the mattress. He must remove them before Roxana discovered them. She would be furious to know that he'd spent many intimate moments lusting after those nude girls and gratifying himself.

"Roxana."

She looked at him.

"I think you should go back to studying. You should go to college."

"I don't mind," she said, munching the muri.

"Maybe next year, when I graduate."

"What will you do after graduation?"

"Get a good job. Then the first thing we will do is move into a bigger and nicer house. With electricity and running water."

Roxana thought about something and broke into a sly smile.

"What?"

"What will we need a bigger house for?"

"Time will tell." He laughed.

They had tea again. They talked about the looming political uproar, their coming days and months, and their future.

—

Shelley yawned. He checked his Timex. 11:50. The night was quiet. Lying in bed, they were looking out of the window. The sky was the color of charcoal gray. The air felt soothing. It might rain, he said. Roxana's head was on his chest, her hand lying on his torso playing with his chest hair.

"Look." She pointed her finger toward the sky.

Shelley asked what it was.

"The eye of a Rakshasa."

He squinted. Up in the sky there was a cloud by the moon shaped like a monstrous eye. He said nothing for a minute, then said, "You're creative."

He kissed her forehead and asked her to go to sleep. "Good night," he said softly. A few minutes later, his eyes fluttered open to find Roxana staring at him, her eyes placid, unblinking.

"Roxana!"

"Mhmm."

"Aren't you sleeping?"

"Tomorrow I have the whole day to sleep."

He touched her check. "Uhhu, sleep now. I'll be back home as early as I can."

"You look adorable in your slumber. Baby-like. You know that?"

"Do I look horrible when I'm awake, then?"

"You look as you are. But cooler when you're asleep. Your belly rises and falls. You snore a little. I love watching you."

He stroked her hair and kissed her.

"Accha, are you sure my father can't find us?"

"Well, the reality is we cannot hide from him for very long. He may now be able to locate us. But isn't it too late? We're legally married. What can he do to us now?"

Roxana exhaled deeply. "My father is impossible, you know. That scares me."

Shelley knew the tall, well-built man with a sharp, powerful gaze that meant you couldn't look him in the eye. Such a man, Shelley had always assumed, might be a tough headman, but could never be a kind husband or a loving father.

"Sleep, babe," he said to Roxana. "We're together."

He pretended to be asleep. But he couldn't keep his mind away from thinking about Roxana's impossible father. A heavy shadow seemed to be hanging over them.

7

The night breeze of Gopala at this time, thought Roxana, should be more pleasant, gentler, and lighter. She wondered what was going on in the village now, after their elopement. What her poor mother was going through. Had Father struck her for her unruly daughter's wrongdoing? She wished she could have kept the innocent woman away from this predicament.

Roxana remembered Nana, Mother's father, who came once a year. Mother had not visited her parental home once after marriage. Father said the husband's home was the real home for women. He frowned on Mother even thinking about her parental home. When talking to Father, Nana's voice was meek, too meek to make any request to his son-in-law. Nana would leave with drowning eyes. And Mother would go without eating anything that day.

For many years, Roxana didn't know her mother had a name. She was always called or addressed as "Roxana's ma." It was only Nana who called Mother "Mini."

On the day of her fleeing, Roxana got up early in the morning. Mother was already in the kitchen, lighting up a fire in the earthen chula. Roxana knelt before her and salaamed her feet.

"What happened?" Mother asked with a start.

"Emnei, nothing," she answered.

The night before, Roxana had barely slept. For a long time she pondered the matter of marrying the Karachi groom. Father's chosen husband, she wondered, would he just be a milder version of her tiger father? Roxana couldn't imagine herself being in the same bed with a stranger. And what would her position be like in his home after some years? Same as her miserable mother? Wouldn't death be worthier than allowing herself to live in that purgatory? She sat up, shaking. Her fingernails dug into her palms, and she said to herself, "If Father kills me for marrying Shelley, let it be."

Roxana took a breath. Now she was the happiest girl on earth. She and Shelley were finally together, under the same roof. In one bed, in each other's arms. She could feel his warm breath, could listen to the cadenced beating of his heart. She buried her nose in his breast. She smelled him, kissed him softly. As she closed her eyes, the sweet, salty taste of his skin lingered in her mouth.

—

Later at night, Roxana woke up sobbing. She was breathing heavily, sweating all over. Stupefied, seized by a chilly sensation. She looked around and realized where she was. She touched Shelley. Nestled against his arm, she held him tight, still shaking.

"Roxana?" Shelley awoke with a start.

Roxana pressed her face into his chest. She felt cold. Her nose was clogged. She had to breathe through her mouth.

"What's wrong, honey?"

"Something," she murmured. "Something strange happened."

"What?"

"Granny!" She held him tighter. After a long while, when she could finally speak, she told Shelley that she had seen her granny's face in the window, her hands holding the two window bars. She had looked exceedingly white in her white blouse and white sari. But her lips were red from chewing paan. She was in tears and telling Roxana to be careful of her tiger son.

"It was real, and I saw it crystal clear," Roxana said.

Just then a house gecko on the wall opened its vocal cords. TICK TICK TICK.

They both peered at the direction of the sound.

"See, even the gecko testifies to this."

Shelley was silent, giving her a strange look. He hugged her, stroked her back. They remained quiet. Then they both looked at the window, at the predawn darkness outside. Somewhere a bird was calling in a mournful tone. A fresh, soft breeze pervaded the room.

Roxana thought of her granny's hand embroidery hanging on the wall in her old room. It was a fine, beautiful stitch of two sitting peacocks. Their beaks held a message: "BHULONA AMAAY." *Forget me not.* Her granny! Dead for two years. She wiped a tear from her eye.

"Roxana, nothing to fear. I'm here with you."

"Granny was always worried about my future."

"Why?"

"Because I was born on a Saturday night. And I had a difficult birth."

"Oh dear, you believe these prejudices?"

"I don't. But I believe my granny."

"Honey, please try to sleep."

—

Early in the morning there was a hammering on the door. It wouldn't stop. It went on and on.

Roxana sat up, startled. She found Shelley already awake, open-eyed.

The banging got louder and louder. A slice of slanting sunlight slipped through the window.

"Don't answer," Roxana whispered, holding his hand.

"Open the door!" said a rough, restless voice with the repeated knocks. "It's the police."

CHAPTER FOUR

1

A name plate on the desk read "Inspector Mahmood Zaman." Sitting behind the desk was the inspector. Above his head was a portrait of the founding father of the country. Clean-shaven, in a Karakul Afghan hat, Muhammad Ali Jinnah watched everything from there.

Standing on the other side of the desk were Roxana and Shelley. She was holding on to Shelley's arm. Inspector Mahmood Zaman's eyes, under his bushy eyebrows, zoomed in on her and then on him.

"Put this malaun in lockup," the inspector said.

One policeman gave Shelley a sharp push, then marched him away.

"Listen to me, listen to me!" Shelley screamed.

Roxana's strong grip on Shelley's arm loosened as another policeman took hold of her.

"Don't touch me!" she cried.

—

Before reaching the lockup, Shelley was punched in the gut. His body curled like a shrimp's. A kick in the backside sent him straight into the pen.

"Bastard malaun," the policeman growled. He shut the lockup door and walked away.

"Fuck you!" Shelley spat. He was on all fours.

There was a little laughter. Shelley swung his head around. Two other men were inside the windowless cell. One was sitting against a wall and smoking, the other was laughing, leaning against the grate. The laughing man, whose grimy face mocked him, looked like a tramp. Shelley turned away.

"Halar hoga dekhsen?" the smoking man said. Had Shelley noticed that police officer's ass? "Like the khankis of Kandupatti."

The tramp cracked up at the mention of the asses of the brothel women in Kandupatti. Shelley eyed the smoking man. His face was expressionless. The man chucked a cigarette and a matchbox toward Shelley. He picked up the cigarette, lit it, and tossed the matches back. He took a long drag just as the tramp broke the silence with a bone-racking cough.

Hot as hell, the lockup reeked of piss and shit. There was a toilet in the corner of the cell. Only smoke masked the odor.

Time slipped by. An hour. More. Suddenly the door opened. The guard yelled at the sleeping tramp to get up. Shelley saw his chance. He begged the guard to bring him news of his wife. The guard paid no attention; he yelled again at the tramp, "Move your ass. you son of a bitch!" Once he shuffled out of the lockup, the door slammed shut.

"You won't get anywhere that way," the smoking man said. He was watching Shelley. "It's a world with a different language. What's your case anyway?"

Perhaps the man could help him. Shelley moistened his lips. "We got married on our own."

"A runaway marriage?"

He nodded.

The man explained to him the facts. Here, words were worthless, only money talked. Did Shelley have any with him? Or tradable items, like cigarettes? Shelley handed him two ten-taka bills. Slowly the man stood, stepped up to the barred door, and, letting his one hand out through the bars, snapped his fingers three times. The guard emerged. He deposited the money in the guard's palm and made clear what Shelley was after.

The answer came two hours later. This time the guard reappeared with a man who had just been arrested. He unlocked the door for the man and delivered his message to Shelley: the girl's uncle had come and taken her away.

So Roxana's chacha uncle had come all the way from Gopala. What were they plotting? The banker in Karachi, the man who had been supposed to marry Roxana, must have dropped out of the deal by now. Were they still going to try and remarry her? In a tight grip, Shelley pulled at the side of his hair. It was so foolish of him to assume that everything would be fine. How, how would he rescue Roxana now? Would he ever see her again? His eyes blurred.

"Do you go to Dhaka University?"

The question came from the new man. His thin face seemed familiar to Shelley. The guy was about his age. Shelley did not respond, but nodded in agreement.

"I've seen you around. I study sociology." He said his name was Habeeb and asked, "What are you in for?"

Why was Shelley here? No, not for political reasons. "No, no," Shelley muttered. He sat down on the floor, holding his head in his hands.

Habeeb told him about his own bad luck. He had been heading to school. In his satchel he was carrying handbills and posters outlining the six-point demand. Near Jagannath College, two policemen stopped him and asked to look in his bag. He ran, but they caught him.

"No one knows I'm here," he said. He wanted to know how things worked at the police station. How long he would have to be in this dump.

Shelley had no clue. Maybe a day. Or two. Or three. A week?

"You scholars have little legal knowledge," the smoking man cut in. Shelley and Habeeb turned. They had forgotten someone else was with them, listening intently.

"The police can't keep anyone in custody for more than twenty-four hours without a judge's order," he said. "They'll take you to court tomorrow. There, you might get bail or be sent back to the cell. Or the magistrate might grant a remand if the police want. Like me. I'm on a three-day remand. I've spent a great deal of time in lockups and jails. Legal things are a child's play to me."

"What did you do anyway?" said Habeeb.

"I'm a dacoit, a bandit," the man said.

Shelley inspected the man. He had a dark unshaven face with a big nose and a thick black mustache. No violent features. This man robbed and looted houses?

"You look pretty normal to me," said Shelley.

"Well, I might be a dacoit, but I'm not a bad man. Even though I killed three people."

Shelley and Habeeb exchanged glances.

"Well, I hate killing. But sometimes in my business you're left with no choice. Either kill or get killed."

2

Lunch arrived. The half-boiled rice, watery lentils, and mashed potatoes looked so terrible Shelley didn't touch his food. Habeeb ate a little. "It tastes like shit," he said. To get rid of the taste in his mouth, he lit a cigarette. The three of them smoked in silence, sitting with their backs against the same wall.

A piercing scream broke the stillness. Shelley straightened up and Habeeb stared. The man was unfazed. "Interrogation," he told them.

The longer the screams continued, the more the silence thickened around them. Shelley thought about the previous day—he had been with Roxana having biryani for lunch. Roxana had wanted him to stop eating restaurant food. Today he could bet she was also going hungry. An intense pain gripped his heart. Shelley should have been taken along with Roxana. He would have begged them to punish him in any way they deemed appropriate. His only request would have been not to torture Roxana.

"Are you a communist?" the man asked Habeeb in a low voice.

Habeeb squinted and darted a glance at Shelley.

Did communists have a distinct look? What made Habeeb any different from him? Habeeb was in a khadi kurta with a mandarin collar over white pajamas. Shelley himself was wearing a cream-colored cotton shirt with khaki pants. Habeeb had a mustache. Shelley did not. Neither of them looked odd or seemed different.

"In case you are," the man continued, "never, ever confess it to the police. You'll end up spending your whole life in jail." He sighed. "I've been in jail many times. First time in 1943. Seven years total. Heard of Trailokyanath Chakravarty? A big British revolutionary. He spent thirty years in jail."

"Thirty years!" Habeeb gave a cry.

"I know," Shelley said. "But did you really meet him?"

"I didn't meet him. I heard his name." A subtle smile spread across his mouth. "The first requirement of a good dacoit is you've got to have good ears. I listen to everything around me and never forget."

Shelley stared at his stony face, the robustly built man in his late forties, puffing on a cigarette.

Just then the sound of boots approached the lockup. The guard called for Habeeb.

"What for?" Habeeb breathed, looking at Shelley. "Interrogation?"

Habeeb's hands were trembling. Shelley gripped his sleeve but couldn't say a word. He let his new friend leave in silence.

"That boy is in trouble." The man turned his gaze on Shelley. "You are not."

The words did not pacify Shelley. He was not perturbed about his potential interrogation. He was worried about the possible torture and torment that Roxana might be enduring. He shook and got chills just thinking about that.

"Let me know if you're hungry, or want to eat something good," the man said. "I've got a hole in my throat. Got gold and money stored in there."

Gold and money stored in his throat? This man must be pulling his leg. A robber, then a triple murderer, then gold in a hole in the throat. Shelley wrinkled his forehead. The man saw his doubt.

"Okay," the man said, turning his face to the wall. He made a horrible retching sound, and a coin came out of his mouth. At last he said, "Now? Some tea?"

It was magic. Shelley thanked him but asked only for a cigarette. The retching sound had left him nauseated. "Why are you a bandit, if you don't mind my asking?"

The man struck a match, lit a cigarette. "I love danger. A job that involves risk. The Gita says choose the work you like. Something you can do well and that suits your nature. I'm following the Gita."

Shelley gazed at the Gita-graduate dacoit. "Are you Hindu?"

"I am."

"Why didn't you move to India after the Partition?"

"A dacoit skin in Pakistan will be the same skin in India. Dacoity is like a war. You need to know your enemies well before you attack. Here I know everything like the back of my hand."

"I doubt it's the teachings of the Gita that brought you into this profession. What's the real story?"

"The real story? Huh, the real story?" After a long silence the man began talking as if he were speaking to himself. Yes, he, Monu Mandal, had a real story. The story of being a dacoit. How old had he been then? Fifteen probably. He had left school years before. He couldn't afford it anymore. The bloody Second World War was on. Life was terrible. Everything got rationed. Then came 1943 and the great famine. Who was Allah? Who was Bhagavan? Rice was the only god. The hoarders, merchants became mightier than God. The young Monu witnessed starving fathers willing to sell their daughters for a few kilograms of rice. In those days, a chicken was more enticing than the flesh of a woman.

For the first time the country saw that men could die from hunger, that money couldn't buy everything. Even people with money had no rice.

During the famine, the young Monu's mother gave birth. Famished, she died asking for rice. The newborn died a few days later. That week Monu formed a gang and looted rice from a hoarder's house. Their success emboldened him, and with his hungry gang he drifted from village to village, town to town. He ended up being a burglar—a dacoit leader. The more challenging the game, the more pleasure it gave him.

—

The sound of footsteps grew louder and halted at the lockup. The guard brought Habeeb back but did not leave. Instead he gestured for Monu to go with him.

Shelley saw one in, one out. The door opened, the door locked.

Habeeb plopped down on the floor. His hair was disheveled, his face puffy with red marks.

Shelley passed him the jug of water. Habeeb nodded slightly. He gulped, let out a big breath, and shut his eyes.

The guard was back again. Was it Shelley's turn now? His heart drummed. Two mazar wanderers entered the lockup. The guard left without asking for Shelley.

Shelley eyed the bizarre newcomers. Their long matted hair and beards. They wore a variety of bracelets; around their scrawny necks were necklaces of wooden beads. Two red unstitched cloth pieces covered their bodies. One was wrapped like a skirt, the other like a shawl. They were neither young nor old. With their jaundiced eyes and uncustomary appearance, they resembled temple sadhus. But while sadhus were principally Hindu, these mazar wanderers were Muslim. No one said a word. Their hands moved back and forth constantly like a cow's tail, to keep away mosquitoes.

Two hours later Monu returned, unconscious. Two guards dropped him down on the lockup floor. Face badly swollen, he had cuts and bruises all over his body. Blood trickled from one corner of his lips, from his broad shoulders, from his knees. The top button of his short-sleeved shirt was missing. The lungi around his waist was lazily wrapping his loins. Shelley put his ear against the Monu's sternum. His heart was beating.

One of the holy wanderers sprinkled some water over his face. Monu's eyes fluttered, and his lips parted a little, as if to say something. Water? Everyone helped him to drink some water.

Long afterward, Monu managed to sit up. He assumed his usual position, his back against the wall. But whenever his head drooped, he resembled a seated corpse. Even so, you could make out every muscle on his sinewy body.

At one point Monu raised his head. He looked up at the two holy wanderers and asked if they could prepare a lump of weed for him. The holy wanderers answered that they did not have any on them.

"You bums live on it. If nowhere on the body, it's hidden in your asshole. Take that crap out. Ganja's good for pain relief."

The two holy wanderers looked at each other. The lanky wanderer winked at his companion, who was short and hollow eyed. Next, the hollow-eyed wanderer took out a teeny wad of weed from one side of his thick matted dreadlocks. Monu passed him two cigarettes. The hollow-eyed wanderer began his craft. His black bony fingers replaced the tobacco with marijuana as if he were performing an arcane ritual. All the while he lamented the loss of his most precious belonging in the world, his chillum pipe. The police had thrown it away when they were busted. He had no idea why the police had brought them here.

The hollow-eyed wanderer finished his craft. He lit one of the weed cigarettes and gave Monu the other to light. Shelley and Habeeb showed no interest in either.

"Tell you what," said Monu, looking over at Shelley and Habeeb, "during the British period, prisoners got more facilities. As I see it, we were better off when the British were here."

"Beyond the shadow of a doubt," agreed Habeeb. "We have the world we deserve. Bengalis are cows tied by the neck. West Pakistanis are happily pulling the rope."

The weed-smoking made the cell quiet and drowsy. But soon a foul-smelling gas flooded the hot and sweaty space, barely leaving room for any oxygen.

"Stop blowing stink out of your shithole," Monu thundered. He threatened those slimy holy bums that if they didn't stop farting, he'd kick the holy hell out of them.

—

The police station was sleepy, and the earth was hushed. Habeeb and the holy bums were asleep on the floor. Monu, too, slumped against the wall. But Shelley was wakeful. Roxana, he thought, must be awake and thinking about him. They both were imprisoned—he in lockup, she in home confinement. What else could he have done to avoid this unlawful arrest? Where else could he have escaped with Roxana?

Somewhere, a dog yowled. Someone swore in the nearby street. And inside the cell the snoring abated. There was no light inside. A lamp outside cast a dull light into the cell.

Something grabbed Shelley's attention. He squinted.

The lanky bum, quiet as a cat, climbed onto his companion's back. Like a lizard on another lizard. His movements, which lasted less than a minute, eased off. Once the lanky bum was done thrusting his pelvis, he rolled off from him. The hollow-eyed bum then mounted him and did the same. Their sharp pleasure ended promptly. Shelley turned his gaze to Monu. Still asleep? Had the silent sodomy gone unnoticed by him? The dacoit had no doubt kept his eyes shut, but his ears open.

Later that night Shelley spotted Monu picking something off the floor and dropping it onto the lanky bum's slumbering body. It was a piece of rubbery roti left over from supper. An army of small ants soon came after it.

For the rest of the night the lanky bum scratched himself all over, his moans drowning out the whine of the mosquitoes.

3

Inspector Mahmood Zaman took no notice of Shelley. At his desk he was writing in a register. The morning sun slanted through one of the windows. Shelley was standing where he'd stood the day before, behind the same chair, next to where Roxana had stood.

The inspector took his time. Before closing the register, he double-checked what he had just written. Then he lifted his head. His glinting eyes under bushy brows held Shelley. He leaned back in his chair. With a kingly gesture, he signaled to Shelley to sit down.

Shelley sat. The inspector had a stern look on his face. A long policeman's stare. A silent interrogation? He noted that the inspector's undershirt was visible. Also visible was his bare hairy chest peeping out from under his white vest.

Men with chest hair were compassionate, affectionate, his ma used to say. "See your baba. He has no chest hair. That's why he is so cold, indifferent."

"Leboo Pagla has thick chest hair. Like wild grass. Then why does he chase children with bamboo?" Shelley asked his ma. He didn't mention that Leboo Pagla had thick pubic hair as well.

Lunatic Leboo Pagla had served in the Second World War in Burma. When he returned home, he left his bravery behind. He freaked out at the sight of blood. So children would walk over to him with battered and bloodied earthworms. That little blood made Leboo Pagla scream and sprint to the rice field.

"Name? Your name?" the inspector asked.

"Shelley."

"Shelley what?"

"Shelley Majumder."

"Hindu?" The words hummed under his presidential mustache.

The president of the country had a gray-and-black chevron mustache. The inspector, in his early forties, had an all-black one.

"I asked a question." said the inspector.

Shelley gave a nod.

"Speak," the inspector barked. His accent sounded northern.

Shelley assumed his origin. West Bengal. A migrant from India. The inspector must have migrated here after the Partition. "Yes. I was born into a Hindu family," Shelley answered.

Another long stare. The inspector twiddled his presidential mustache. "Where do your parents live?"

"Gopala."

"All your family?"

"My father lives in Gopala. My mother and two sisters are in India."

"What the hell are you doing here, then? Why don't you get your ass over there?"

Shelley had expected this. It was the same question he answered many times for many people. "They moved there because of the riots. My mother did it for my sisters' safety."

"Fair enough. Hindus will move to Hindustan, Muslims to Pakistan. That's what the Partition was for. So why didn't you move?"

"I am a Hindu. But I was born here. In East Bengal. East Pakistan."

"But you are Hindu. A Hindu can't love Pakistan. I know you Hindus well. You guys get education here. Work here. But smuggle all your wealth to India. Seen it a lot."

The words whipped Shelley. Nobody had ever said that to his face before.

"But that's not my concern here," the inspector continued. "My concern is, how dare you do hanky-panky with a Muslim girl?"

Hanky-panky? Shelley stared at him. "We are legally married. I converted to Islam."

"Heh!" A sudden flood of air bubbled out of the policeman's mouth. He half rose from his chair, brought his furious police face close to Shelley's. "Don't you talk law with me. I keep law in my pocket. Understood?"

Shelley understood.

"You converted to Islam, eh?" The inspector glared at Shelley. "Are you circumcised yet? No? You are still a Hindu. A malaun."

Malaun? Accursed? In the Land of the Pure, Hindus were accursed? A vulgar rhyme from the 1964 riots vibrated in Shelley's memory: *Grab Hindus by one and two, nibble 'em in the fore and afternoon, too.*

Muslim rioters used it a lot back then. Shelley, for several days and nights, had had nightmares about this horrific rhyme. They would skin him like a chicken? Like a goat? Roast him for dinner? Many bloodcurdling stories of murder seeped into Gopala at the time of the riots. Muslim rioters in Khulna hijacked trains. They checked every male passenger's penis and killed on the spot anyone who was uncircumcised.

The inspector stood up. He sidestepped Shelley, reached for the empty chair on Shelley's left. Shelley felt tiny next to this large policeman. The inspector lifted his left leg and put his foot on the edge of the chair. He bent forward. His pudgy fingers went for his boot. For the loosened laces.

The policeman's boot shone like a knife. You could see your face in it. The inspector had hairy forearms. His fingers unfastened the loosened knot first. Then he made two loops, crossed one over the other, and pulled one through the bottom hole away from the other. Finally he smoothed the front loop.

"Look, you'll remember me your whole life. For the favor I will do you." The inspector returned to his chair and observed Shelley for some reaction to his words. "You walk free from here. No charge. No court. Nothing. Just one small condition."

Shelley looked straight at the inspector.

"Never again contact the girl. Never means *never*. In your entire life, never. Bury your feelings. Forget it ever happened. If you can promise me that, you are free to go. Now."

A pause.

"What do you think?"

"I can't forget her," Shelley said.

"I'll give you another chance. Think hard."

"I can't forget. Not till I die."

"Let me end your life then," the inspector hooted with pleasure. "I was trying to be nice. Seems you want to drag me into this dirty affair." He paused and grew serious again. "Listen, you can never get that girl back. You need to understand what will happen if you try to see her again."

"I don't care."

"You will care. The real trouble begins when I send you to court. Are you ready for that?"

"I am."

"That's that, then."

The inspector called to someone. The same policeman who had brought Shelley here emerged from a side door.

"Send him to court."

"Yes, sir." The policeman seized Shelley's arm.

"Hold on," Shelley said, thinking fast. "I accept your condition."

The inspector motioned for the policeman to leave again.

"You mean it?" He glanced at Shelley suspiciously.

"I mean it." The consequence didn't matter. He needed to get out to see Roxana.

"Don't fuck with me," the inspector said. "I'll make your life worse than hell. Put you under the Security Act. You know what that means. As an enemy of the state, you'll spend the rest of your life in prison."

Shelley looked up at the portrait above the inspector's head. Had the man not migrated from India, there would have been a different portrait over his head. A portrait of nonviolence.

"I understand," Shelley said.

4

It was dark. Gopala was in repose. Picking his way through in the hazy moonlight, Shelley made for Laloo's home, Chowdhury's cowshed. Past Chowdhury's pond, the family graveyard, the lychee tree, the mango-jackfruit grove, he reached the yard at last. The cowshed, adjoining a hill of straw, was too big for three cows. He sneaked in. Across from him, the reclining cows were calm, uninterested. At the mouth of the shed he found Laloo, asleep on the straw. The minute he kneeled to wake him, Laloo opened his eyes and sat up.

"Come along," Shelley said under his breath.

Away from the cowshed, he stopped by a clump of bamboo. Here the sound of crickets was shattering the night. He saw Laloo trailing behind, his steps short, slow.

"Laloo, why are you limping?"

No answer.

"What happened?"

"They beat me."

"Who beat you?"

"But me said nothing."

Shelley squatted, felt Laloo's limping foot. It was the ankle, awfully swollen. "Who beat you, Laloo?"

"It doesn't hurt."

True. A beating never hurt Laloo. Before the pain started, he would think of something else. An old trick. He had mastered the art of absorbing beatings when he was a little boy.

The evening Roxana went missing, Laloo began to tell Shelley, they had tied him to a betel nut tree. They claimed he knew everything. That he knew Shelley and Roxana were going to flee the village. Shelley could not have done it without his assistance.

"Why didn't you tell us beforehand?" they asked him, beating him with bamboo sticks.

What stupid accusations! How was he supposed to know Shelley and Roxana were planning to run away? Shelley had never told him. All Shelley said was: "Roxana and I are doing something serious this time." That didn't mean anything. And even if he did suspect the two were leaving, why would he inform the others? In his experience, talking only caused trouble. The more you talked, the more trouble you created. Besides, Shelley was his only human friend. How could he betray his buddy, reveal his secrets?

Hunchbacked Hawlader grunted. "Beating this idiot is a waste of time. This dumbass wouldn't talk if you threw him in a fire."

"Problem is he's gullible. He does whatever he's told. Shelley's the main scoundrel, not him." Hawlader then reminisced about how Laloo's father had been a marvelous idiot, too. And not just his father. Actually, fourteen generations of Laloo's family had been idiots.

They tired themselves out beating him, and Roxana's chacha left for the police station in town.

"Bloody idiot," Hawlader said, dropping the bamboo stick. "He should have been born a cow. At least then he would have been useful."

They untied Laloo. He had to half crawl to reach Chowdhury's cowshed. His wife, Lali, cried to see him in that awful state. She licked him all over with her big tongue. The licking comforted him. It took two days for him to get back on his feet.

Then on the day Roxana was brought back to Gopala, they locked her up. Old Baari consented to marry her. He was newly widowed. It didn't matter that he was old enough to be Roxana's father and had two sons older than her. A Muslim, an important family name—that was what mattered. Of course, the marriage included a fat dowry from Roxana's father. Who would marry the runaway girl otherwise?

Shelley spent the rest of the night alone on the riverbank. The day was breaking when he entered his home through the front yard. Baba saw him from his bedroom window and opened the door. For a moment they stood silent. Shelley, looking at the ground, said, "I'm sorry."

Baba sighed. "Go wash yourself. Eat something and take a rest. We'll talk later."

Shelley slowly walked to his room. After a quick wash in the pond, he changed into a lungi and undershirt. He ate puffed rice with date syrup, and then lay in bed looking out the window.

Throughout the night he had pondered his next move. He wanted to run to Baari's and reclaim Roxana right away. He cried. He couldn't bear the thought that old Baari was sleeping next to her, and his old hands were touching her. He almost decided to burn down Baari's house. But he composed himself. There must be a way to rescue Roxana, he said to himself as he pulled his hair.

—

When the maid called him for lunch the next day, Shelley said he was not hungry. Baba came to his room and stood by the bed. Shelley sat up.

"You let me down," Baba said. "Roxana's father stopped in after the day you left. I don't want to get into the details of how he threatened and humiliated me. It was . . . it was—" Baba bit into his lip and couldn't speak for a moment.

Shelley met his glance for a second. "I'm sorry, Baba."

Baba took a breath. "You know, it's not easy when you set to swim against the current," he said. "But at least you tried. I am sorry to see that your plan didn't work out."

"My advice is," he said after a silence, "return to Dhaka tomorrow. Get back to your studies and work. You do that, and I will forgive you." Baba paused. "It's hard, I know, but believe me, you will be okay. And for god's sake, don't do anything stupid this time. Roxana is someone else's wife now."

Shelley remained silent. A rooster crowed outside.

"Come," Baba said before leaving the room. "Lunch's getting cold."

—

It was not long after dusk when Laloo's face appeared at his window. "This is for you," he said, holding out a folded paper for Shelley.

Shelley jumped out of bed. "Who gave you this?"

Laloo said in whispers that a servant girl from Roxana's house had told him to pass it to Shelley.

Shelley opened the letter before the hurricane lamp. The handwriting, hurried and hazy, was surely Roxana's.

> *I know you will be in Gopala to look for me. One thing I want to assure you about is that I am fine here. Though it's late, but I realized that I made a mistake. We do not live only for ourselves; we live for others as well. If we think about only our own pleasure and happiness, the world will be a terrible place.*

You know I grew up in an affluent family. I don't think I could have lived in your small, dilapidated place in Dhaka for long. My present husband, Baari, is rich, and I will be happy here.

I want no more trouble (have already gone through enough). Please do not try to contact me. Nothing will change my mind.

—R

Shelley crumpled up the letter and hurled it across the room.

5

The next morning, Shelley caught the train to Dhaka. As the train jolted into action, it struck him that it was Thursday. Last week it had been Tuesday when Roxana and he had left Gopala together. He had had a five-day married life. And now Roxana was someone else's wife. He buried his trembling face in his hands.

It was a hot day, and the carriage was packed. Shelley was sweating profusely.

"How far?" he asked the traveler next to him.

"Dhaka? That's close. About an hour or so away."

He puffed out with a groan and held his head with his hands. The unending rocking and creaking, the constant swaying and clattering was splitting his skull open.

"Are you okay?"

Shelley didn't answer.

When the train slowed and stopped at Fulbaria Station, Shelley pushed past throngs of passengers, making his way out to an uncrowded place. He was gasping for air. He stood leaning against a beam at the platform. He crouched low, clawing his churning stomach, and spewed up food. Everything around him was spinning. The noise, the people, the train whistle—all appeared to him a mirage. The sounds around him seemed to be coming from a distance. He lingered for a while. From an adjoining tea stall outside, he had some water and milk tea. Then he flagged down a rickshaw.

Unlocking the front gate to his home, Shelley spotted a note from Manick. *Been worried sick. Come see us ASAP.* He opened the door to his room and stood motionless. He could picture the morning he and Roxana had been lying on the bed. He walked over to the clothes stand and ran his fingers over Roxana's dress, still draped there. He sniffed it hard.

He was hungry, but he had no appetite. There was a tutoring job he needed to attend. He decided to visit Manick instead. The night was falling. Shelley showered in the dark. He dressed up, lit a cigarette, and stepped outside.

—

Manick opened the gate and cried out, "Shelley!" He touched his shoulder. "Come, come. Do you know how many times I visited your house? I even went to your magazine office. No one knew anything of you. You just vanished."

As they approached the living room, Shelley saw Maya hurry down the stairs.

"Shelley!" she said.

They all sat in the living room.

"Why do you look—?" Maya stopped midsentence.

"What happened to you, Shelley?" Manick said. "You were supposed to be back in a week. It's been now, what? Over two weeks?"

Shelley glanced at Manick and Maya. "Roxana," he said. "Roxana's gone."

—

In the second week of September, Shelley received a letter from Baba. It was dated September 3, 1968. Roxana, Baba wrote, died last Monday. She had had a fever for over a week. He attached another letter that came from Roxana. It had been handed to him by her servant girl. The edges of the folded letter were glued together. Shelley broke the letter open.

I don't know whether this letter will ever reach you. Even if it does and by the time you will read it, I may not be breathing anymore. I'm very sick and weak, so weak that I'm struggling to hold the pen straight. You can see how bad my handwriting is.

Most of the time I'm half awake or half asleep. And what do I do? I write you letters in my mind, all the time. Don't you receive them? If I'm not writing, I am talking to you, or I am thinking about you. Accha, have you believed everything that I said in my previous letter? I wrote that so you could start hating me. At least a little. Thought that might help you forget me for a time. What else could I have done? Father said if I tried anything again, he'd kill me and throw my body into the river. And you would never come out of jail. No, I wasn't scared of death; all I cared about was your safety. So I complied. You once told me that love is being selfless, being one heart in two bodies. We may be worlds apart now, but we're two flowers on one stem.

You may have many questions about my marriage to Baari. I could have stopped it for sure, killing myself. Then I thought, what if my death causes you and your baba further trouble? So I yielded. No, I didn't let old Baari touch me. I spent a night with him in the same room, yes. When he came, I warned him, "I'll hang myself if you touch me." While old Baari slept in bed, I spent the night sitting in a chair by the corner window, reminiscing about our time in Dhaka.

We had such a wonderful time! Good times are always short-lived, and that's why they are good. Would you believe I haven't had a proper meal since we parted that morning? Now my stomach has shrunk so surprisingly that it cannot bear any intake anymore. Whatever I consume, within five minutes I throw it up. Even water.

Yes, they give me meds. I pretend to swallow, but as soon as they are out of sight, I spit those out. What is the point of living a life without you anyway?

I see Granny these days quite often. She smiles at me and says that I don't have to suffer long. My time is close. That's the reason I thought I should write you a last letter. At this moment, I've no hard feelings against anyone. No hate, no desire, no expectation. Nothing. Oh, maybe a small wish. Only if I could lie on your chest just one more time.

Remember, you once gave me Sarat Chatterjee's Srikanta? There is one beautiful line toward the end of the first part: "Great love not only unites but also separates." Ours is great love, isn't it? Now I can love you more from afar.

Stay good. If you keep well, I'll be well.

—R

PART
TWO

CHAPTER FIVE

1

On the night Shelley first left for Gopala, Maya couldn't sleep. She had a headache. She stayed out on the front balcony for a long time, reclining in the rattan armchair.

The night was warm. The half-moon was still and low in the sky. Some distant stars blinked at her. For no reason, her eyes welled up. Was she upset about Shelley's impending marriage? No, why should she be? She knew, had known all along, that Shelley had a sweetheart. But here in Dhaka he lived a life of unbroken regularity, without surprises or intruders. Now he was going to marry. She wondered what the girl was like. In a week or so, Shelley would be here again, not alone this time. A girl, in the role of a wife, would be sticking to him like an ever-present shadow. Maya breathed deeply. She realized she still had no friends in this town. No one she could talk to.

The night watchman blew his whistle. And then his voice shrieked, piercing the slumbering dead world. *Beware! Beware!*

Every so often Maya imagined inviting the watchman to join her for a cup of tea. As the night matured, he was the only one who could be taken for her soulmate. For they both breathed the thick night air. She had never seen his face. But she could single out his nocturnal voice, even among the ghosts. Didn't the man ever get scared? Maybe she could go talk and take a walk with him for a while.

Some long nights, she wished she could have slept like her father. "I'm not feeling well," he'd said early one evening and clambered into bed. That was it. That was his last sleep, the last night of his life, on the last day of December 1965. He never woke up to the new year.

Yes, at night she tossed and turned in bed, waking and walking, dreaming and drowning, and whatnot. Her nights were filled with tea, migraines, and, at times, poetry.

Maya sighed. A slow grin spread over her face. She recalled the previous year, 1967. That was the first day they had all gone out together—she, Shelley, and Manick. It was the twenty-first of February. Language Martyrs' Day. She had a pre-sunrise cold shower and put on a white sari. Shelley arrived shortly after dawn was beginning to replace the dark. He was wearing a dove-white kurta, as was her brother. The three drank tea and set off.

The morning breeze of early spring was thick with the fragrance of mango flowers. She swallowed some air, and for the first time in many years she felt that a fresh day was like a fresh life.

Near Dhaka Medical College there was a sea of people. Maya had been to the medical college a couple of times. The Language Martyrs' Memorial stood next to it, now flooded by faces ahead and behind, right and left. People brushing past in every direction. Children chirping like morning birds. And flowers—sundry fresh flowers all over. Hands carrying flowers looked like walking flower plants. And a mythical aroma was hovering in the air.

She was amused, astounded. She hadn't seen or been out in such a massive celebration gathering in Dhaka since she arrived about four years ago. She was glad that Shelley had planned this outing. She glanced up at Shelley and met his eye.

With red roses in hand, they waited in the serpentine line to reach the main monument. It took an hour to pay homage to the language heroes—the heroes who had been killed in 1952 on this day. For they had brought out a procession, demanding that Bengali should be the official language of East Pakistan.

Beware! Beware! The watchman's knifelike words cut the quiet night into pieces. The voice in the wave of echoes kept breaking in the air. Maya rose. Her back was stiff from sitting too long. She went inside to try to get some sleep. As she opened the almirah, she was overcome by the scent of naphthalene. She pulled on a nightie, and a snow-white shriveled mothball fell out. Maya was fond of the mothball smell. She always kept a fresh pack in case she ran out. She would even put a couple under her pillow. Whenever she got horrible headaches, she would sniff them.

She ripped open the fresh packet of mothballs. They resembled tasty lozenges. She sniffed them. They smelled strong, savory, and a little bitter.

What are you waiting for? they said, sneering at her. *Eat us.*

She ate one. And another. Then another.

—

Manick brought in a doctor in the morning.

"How many naphthalene balls did you eat?" asked the doctor.

Maya glanced at the clock on the living room wall. It had struck eight just seven minutes ago. The doctor was in a short-sleeved cream-colored shirt and jet-black pants, both completely wrinkle free. His receding hair had the hue of cigarette ash. She recognized his face. Her brother had once fetched him when their mother fell ill.

"Three," responded Manick for her.

The doctor heard, but asked again. "Three?"

Looking down, Maya nodded. Doctors liked to get the details right by repeating questions. She was certain Manick had already told him everything. The number of mothballs she had eaten the previous night and all its consequences.

"Let me check your tongue." The doctor leaned forward.

She opened her mouth.

"Tongue out." He touched her chin, pulled it up and down. "Okay. Now look at me." His forefinger landed on her cheekbone. Left one, then right one.

Maya caught a whiff of soap from his hand.

"How are you feeling now?" he asked.

"Fine."

"No sickness?"

She shook her head.

"Have you had your breakfast?"

She shook her head again.

The doctor unlatched his bag and dug out a pad and a pen.

"Name?"

Manick told him her name.

"Age?"

"Twenty-two," Manick said.

She watched the doctor's fingers move over the pad. He handed the prescription to Manick and rose.

For breakfast Maya poured herself a cup of tea. After two sips she felt as if a serpent were coiled inside her, and the nausea returned. The naphthalene mothballs still seemed to be hiding in the pit of her stomach. They made her insides rumble, retch. She threw up. The worst thing happened last. She battled for breath, like from an asthmatic attack.

2

Maya remembered the day Shelley had first been introduced to her by Manick. Despite his name, Shelley did not look very smart. He was a pretty regular guy with a shyish, boyish face.

He began to see her more often on his visits. He would tell her about his village, his grandpa. She savored his stories. She, too, would share amusing stories about her life. One drizzly day she told him about an elderly couple who had lived right next door to their Park Circus house back in Kolkata.

The husband was Hindu, the wife an Anglo-Indian Christian. They were always together. Went out together. Came home together. Bought groceries together. Early every evening, Maya would wait by the window to see them returning home from their daily walk. They had three children. One became a Hindu, one a Christian, and the last one practiced Islam.

"Sounds like anarchy," Shelley remarked. "I bet if they had another child, he would have become a Buddhist."

"Everyone thought so."

"What a peculiar family!"

"But there was love in the family."

"I bet there was."

Silence.

"Love," he said absently. "What is love, really?"

"To me," Maya said with a sigh, "love is . . . love is a life that makes you want to live."

—

Some years earlier, Maya recalled, she was excited about her long-awaited marriage. It was a typical Kolkata morning in January 1964. She and her groom-to-be, Rashid, were out buying her wedding sari. They ambled along Market Street. They were a little early. The clothes shops had yet to open. From a street vendor, Rashid bought some bloodred roses. Maya's favorite.

"You will buy me red orchids when we go to Shimla, won't you?" Maya said. She was in all red: red dress and red lips.

"Of course, I will. And purple tulips."

"I can't wait. Honeymoon in Shimla. Ohh!"

"It's too cold there now. Snowing."

"Can't wait to see snow. It must be exciting."

Rashid smiled playfully.

Maya remembered the letter Rashid had sent her the previous year from Shimla, where he trained for his job. "There's nothing sadder than watching the snow fall, all alone on a cold winter's night," he wrote.

Snow. Alone. Cold. Winter. Night.

When she uttered each word one by one, they sounded exotic. Each word weighed more than a sentence. They had a sorrowful, heart-twisting sound.

At that time, she was recovering from typhoid. She canceled her plans to apply to university that year and moved her marriage forward.

Maya searched for something different, not a traditional bridal sari. "Why does a wedding sari always have to be red? Why not pink or purple?"

"What kind of question is that?" Rashid said. "Bengali bridal dresses are always red."

They had a tiff, a slight argument. She acquiesced and picked a dark-red Dhakai jamdani.

Maya and Rashid. They had grown up together in the same neighborhood. She was four years younger than him. Early on, they had loved each other and known that one day they would get married.

Maya could not have imagined then that there would be no wedding. No honeymoon whatsoever.

3

Shelley had once told Maya that she resembled Marilyn Monroe. She had loathed Marilyn Monroe from then on. She did not want to resemble anyone. However, once or twice she wondered about the dark-brown mole. What if she cut it off?

Maya giggled at the absurdity. These kinds of thoughts could drive a person insane. And she had many. When she spent afternoons on the rooftop, she often felt a strong desire to jump. Ever since she was a child, she had relished watching things fly through the air. She used to throw hundreds of things off the roof. Gravity fascinated her still. What would it feel like if she jumped? She might die. But that was not the point of jumping. What she was hoping to experience was the momentary weightlessness of freedom.

Another example. She frequently felt a strong desire to strip and walk around the house naked. Being naked was being *you*, wasn't it? Wanting to be naked was wanting to be free. Free from the clothes people covered you with to define you as one of them. Why be one of them?

Maya's father knew his daughter was crazy. In 1964, after she returned from the hospital in late February, the year of the Kolkata riots, Maya did not talk much.

Father announced one day that he had decided to move to East Pakistan for Maya.

"A bad move," Manick objected. "That country has no future."

"How can you be so sure?"

"What can you expect from a military president? Besides, they're all bloodsuckers, robbing the East."

"I know the politics. But I'm a father."

Since he was her father, how could he sleep at night while his daughter lay awake? Since he was her father, how could he eat and burp while his daughter lived on nothing but tea? If only there was something he could do to stop the past from haunting her forever.

"Don't worry about me," Maya told her father one night. "I will go mad. Sooner or later."

But before the year ended, he agreed to exchange property with a Hindu businessman from Dhaka. The businessman would move into their Park Circus house, and his family would take over the businessman's house in Dhaka. He had no doubt the Dhaka air would bring a change in Maya.

In due course, he moved the family to Dhaka so his daughter could sleep soundly, in a new home and in a new city.

Maya's father knew making money as a lawyer in an unfamiliar city would take time. To make ends meet, he bought two clothing stores in New Market and rented them out.

Sitting on the veranda of Dream Garden, her father would drink tea and smoke tobacco and sigh away the days. The clouds of smoke around him got bigger, and his sighs grew longer. Looking at his face, Maya could tell his mind was elsewhere. Far away in his old beloved city. Lost in his sweet home. Missing his loving friends. His familiar courthouse in Alipore. Everything.

Two months after their arrival, Maya was admitted to Eden College. She sat alone in the back of the class. When class started and the teachers lectured, her eyelids felt heavy. One day, the home economics teacher noticed.

"You come from Kolkata, right? Are all Kolkata girls like you? Do they sleep in class?"

"Actually—" Maya coughed, rising.

"What? Are you up all night changing nappies?"

The class howled with laughter.

"She's unmarried, ma'am," a student volunteered.

"No husband to keep you awake? No babies to wet the bed? So what makes you such a night owl?"

Maya stood silent.

After that incident Maya learned to daydream with her eyes open. During lectures she mentally traveled back to Kolkata. Often, she returned to her old school. She remembered the time her science teacher was in a rage. Why wouldn't she be? None of the students had done the homework assignment. Except Maya. Every other sixth-grade student was made to stand up. Only she was still sitting. Alone.

At her old school, Maya recalled, their English teacher, Miss Rani, was extraordinarily pretty. At the Durga Puja festival during ninth grade, Maya and her friend Deepika went to the English teacher's house. Miss Rani lived close to Park Circus Maidan. She served them some snacks. They liked the coconut laddoos.

"Why isn't Miss Rani getting married?" Maya asked Deepika after they left.

"Goodness! She's a widow. Didn't you know that?"

"I know. But why isn't she getting married again? We Muslims do that."

"We Hindus don't."

"Why? It's completely legal." Maya couldn't recollect the exact year when the British had passed this law.

"Huh. The reality is different."

Maya felt for her English teacher. Such a noble face you could worship her, imagine her a Durga Goddess.

"Well, you know what," Deepika said, "if I were a boy, I'd have married her. I wouldn't have listened to anyone's objections."

After visiting Miss Rani, Deepika did not invite Maya home. Her grandmother had just arrived from Burdwan to celebrate Puja. Deepika's grandmother was caste conscious and disliked Muslims coming into the house. The first time Maya met her, she'd had a lousy experience. Maya and Deepika were gossiping in Deepika's bedroom when she strolled in.

"Who is it, Deepika? Aw, your friend."

She started quizzing Maya. Where she lived, how many siblings she had, what her father did. As soon as the grandmother realized Maya was not Hindu, she screamed in fright, "Ey, you are Muslim? Ram Ram! You should've told me sooner."

Later, Deepika told Maya that her grandmother had changed the bedsheets shortly after Maya left.

"Why?" asked Maya. "I only sat on your bed."

Deepkia apologized. She said the rest of her family was not like her grandmother. Her grandmother was paranoid about losing her caste.

That had been a lifetime ago.

A smile cracked Maya's face. Those golden olden days! Still fresh in her memory. Who knew where Deepika was living now, or where her other schoolmates were. Naturally, they would all be married with children. Would she ever see them again? How could she? They were in India. She was in East Pakistan.

4

The flower of sadness has a strong scent. Pure and powerful, like gardenia. Once the perfume saturates your senses, you can't get over it. From miles away, light years away, the intense and intoxicating fragrance shadows you like a ghost.

Rashid. Maya's would-be groom. That day in January 1964, on the day of his disappearance, the morning dawned in Kolkata, warm and delightful. Hours later, something changed. People began to utter unpleasant things. Fear showed on their faces, in their eyes. Trouble was in the air; the wind began to smell strange.

Riot, riot, they whispered.

"It's all because of the stolen hair."

"Killing for hair?"

"It's the Prophet's hair. From the shrine. It matters."

"It's been found already."

"Who cares? It's an excuse to start a riot. Muslims thirst for Hindus' blood. Hindus thirst for Muslims'."

The riots started like a wildfire, gripped Kolkata. Park Circus was a safe neighborhood for Muslims. Hindu rioters didn't have the guts to enter there.

Rashid, as usual, had left home for the office in the morning. The day ended, but he didn't come home.

Evening turned into night. Horrific stories of bloodshed swirled around. Hindus killing Muslims. Muslims killing Hindus. As if both were making human sacrifices to satisfy their own gods.

At the end of January 1964, Kolkata finally calmed. Life returned to normal once again.

But Rashid never came back.

Nor did his body.

Maya knew he was alive. She knew. She waited and waited. She kept peering through the window at the street below. She stopped sleeping. What if Rashid came and called her in the depths of the night? And what if, finding her slumbering, he left again? Her eyes forgot to blink. They went numb, as if they were small glass marbles. She stopped eating and talking, too.

"Maya, my little girl. Drink this cup of milk," her mother implored. "Two days you haven't eaten anything."

Maya sat unmoved.

"My little good girl. Drink a little." Her mother touched Maya's head.

Maya jerked her head away. "Who are you?"

"Maya! It's me. Your mother. Don't you recognize me? Don't you? Don't you?"

She didn't. Two days later they admitted her to the Institute of Psychiatry.

CHAPTER SIX

1

The ninth grader of St. Francis Xavier's School was not home. Shelley tutored her for an hour four days a week. Leaving the student's house on Larmini Street, he strolled toward Hatkhola Road. He noticed a knot of onlookers. A man was holding a roadside show with his monkey. The monkey on a leash performed tricks, dancing to the beating of a small hand drum. The audience guffawed sporadically. Shelley moved off.

He parked himself before a street magazine corner. He flipped through a few of the magazines. There were some good secondhand books on sale, too, but he lacked the appetite to take a peek. He sighed and turned away.

The afternoon was nice. Shelley thought of going to Manick's but didn't feel like walking in that direction. Maybe he should head for Madhur Canteen to have a little adda with his friends. He had not hung around with them in quite a while, discussing politics. But he didn't like to be in crowds.

A screeching parrot flew overhead. He looked up to see the bird. The sky was cloudless. He heard an incessant blaring sound. A beige Volkswagen ahead of him was honking. The young man at the wheel stuck his head out of the car window and shouted, "You forgot your eyes at home?" Shelley found himself almost in the middle of the street. As the car passed him, he heard the man say, "Idiot!" The girl next to the man in the front seat was laughing. Right then Shelley grabbed a piece of broken brick from the roadside and raised his fist. His arm slowly came down as it struck him that somewhere in her face there was a resemblance between the girl and Roxana. He couldn't tell how. At the tea stall across the street, he smoked and drank tea and thought more about the girl. But all he could remember now was the way she had laughed. Then he quietly listened to the conversations of the other customers around him.

Shelley started walking, sauntering around the streets. When the dusk was falling, he entered Ramna Park. Some joggers were heading out. He looked at an elderly man with a walking stick who reminded him of his baba. A group of boys, sweaty and unwashed after playing football, were enjoying jhalmuri.

Shelley sat on the grass by the lake and lit a cigarette. He watched the owl-light shroud the ground, the water. Soon the evening chorus of birds came to an end, and the park nearly emptied out. A brooding silence hovered about. Shelley stretched out and lay on his back. As he watched the sky change colors, he wondered what life would have been like if nothing had happened to Roxana, and they were still a couple together.

He recalled that the other day Maya had asked him how he was holding up. After an awful storm, he told her, there was always a strange quietness in nature, amid the signs of destruction and uprooted trees all around. All the living beings on earth then remained in a limbo for a while. Maya gave him a stare and said she did understand what he meant.

He heard a soft sound. He spotted the moving figure of a woman nearby. Shelley peered at her and turned his head away. The woman realized he couldn't be her potential customer. After she disappeared behind some tree, he thought he should have paid her to keep him company.

2

He was drowning. The ferocious tide kept dragging him into the deep river. The sky, inky black, roared with thunder. Against the wild waves his body was failing. The river, as vicious as a kalboishakhi storm, threatened to tear him apart. He was losing the battle.

It took Shelley a long moment to sense he was not sinking. He found himself within the four walls of his familiar room, curled up in bed, dream-torn. He couldn't make out whether it was night or morning. But it was raining. His room was illuminated for a second by a flash of a lightning.

The rain continued, getting heavier. Shelley watched the rainfall, the sodden morning through the window. He savored every rhythm, but after a while the sound became monotonous. It sounded like the cry of the sky.

These days he woke in the wee hours of the morning. Some days it was from a dream; some days it was from dryness in the mouth. Some days it was from a pressure to unload his bladder. But he wouldn't get up. Drenched in languor, he would lie still, staring at the low ceiling.

Shelley glanced at his cigarette pack sitting on the desk. He didn't feel like climbing off the bed to collect it. He drew the kantha quilt up to his waist and closed his eyes. He tried to recall the smell of Roxana.

When he woke up next, it was still raining. His stomach rumbled. He checked his watch. 09:22. Still his body refused to get out of bed. He looked at the pile of old magazines next to the cot. On top, an issue of *Filmfare*. The faces of two smiley stars on the cover, eye to eye, lips almost touching. He gazed at the cover, hoping to hear their amorous breathing. He drew a book from the side of his pillow. *The Poems of John Donne*.

The downpour ceased after eleven. He should go to work, to North Brook Hall Road. He got out of the bed and drained two glasses of water.

Sitting on the desk were bread and bruised bananas for breakfast. He fired up a cigarette and decided to go nowhere today.

An hour later Manick was in his room. He put a carrier bag on his desk and said, "Maya sent you some food."

"How did you know I am home?" Shelley asked.

"Friday and a rainy day. Thought you must be slacking off." Manick straddled the chair. "Is everything all right?"

Shelley shrugged.

"Did you talk to your supervisor? About your missed lectures and tutorials?"

Shelley nodded. "He advised to study hard and not to worry."

"That's generous. Good to see you're back in the saddle."

Back in the saddle? Shelley thought. He didn't say he found no reason why he ought to live like others.

"You okay?" Manick asked.

He sighed and nodded.

"You've gone very quiet, Shelley." Manick paused. "Don't suffer in silence. We are here for you, okay?"

He nodded again.

Manick said he should not keep to himself. "It's been a while since you saw friends." He paused and said he was headed to Madhur Canteen. "Come, let's go hang out."

"Not today, thank you," Shelley said.

3

On Sunday afternoon at Dream Garden, Shelley was listening to a Beatles song.

"Over the week," Maya said, browsing through *Begum*, "you've played this song over fifty times."

Shelley knew she had an ear for music. Wherever she was in the house, her ears could pick up every tune the recorder played. She wouldn't miss even the tunes that drifted in from the neighborhood. She'd taken, long ago, lessons in Tagore's music.

"You want another tea?" Maya said. "I'm going to refill mine."

"Sure," Shelley said.

Maya got up. She grabbed her plain, white porcelain mug and made her way to the kitchen. She always kept her hands occupied. Either by the tea mug or the embroidery hoop or something else. And in between, from time to time, she would bite her nails.

Shelley had his eyes shut, resting his head sideways of the sofa. Just then he heard someone shout.

"Salil!"

Aware of the voice that penetrated the living room, Shelley pretended not to hear. He knew who it was—Manick's mother. She always muddled his name.

"Salil!"

Shelley opened his eyes. Manick's mother had already seated herself in the room and began her knitting. He straightened his back and salaamed her.

"Everything good with you, son?" she asked.

"Everything good, auntie." Shelley turned off the record player.

Shelley waited, watched her knit. A half-finished burgundy jumper on her knees. She usually talked about the same thing each time she visited.

"Where do your mother and sisters live in Kolkata? I forgot," she started.

"Shyamnagar."

"Shyamnagar. Good. Good area."

He kept watching her knit. After a few stitches she would talk again.

"We lived in Park Circus." A pause. "You know Lady Brabourne College?"

"I know. But I've never been there," he said.

"Our house was close to the college. Khan Cottage."

"Manick told me."

She exhaled, then inhaled. Then began the tale of her Kagzi lemon tree, her pet tree. She spoke with her clear Calcatian lilt.

"Its flowers had fantastic fragrance. Sweet lemony air floated around. At night I slept breathing in that air. The leaves had a good scent, too. Tasted good with mashed green mangoes in summer."

Shelley recalled the taste of mashed green mangoes with lemon leaves. It made his mouth water. During the dog days in Gopala, it was a daily summer treat.

"You are feeling better now?" she said.

He nodded.

"Death happens, you know. It's not in our hands."

Shelley sighed.

"You became a Muslim, na?"

He looked up and nodded.

"Good, good," she said, "very good."

Another few more stitches, then she spoke again. "Where do your mother and sisters live in Kolkata, you said?"

He repeated the answer.

"Good, good area. We lived in Park Circus. You know that area?"

At that, Manick popped into the room. "What're you doing here, Amma?"

"Uhh . . . talking. I was telling Shelley about our house . . . my lemon tree."

"I think he knows that already." Manick shot Shelley a glance. "Shelley, come to my room a minute."

Shelley followed Manick into his room. Besides a few bookshelves, Manick lived in a relatively small room. Of all his books, most prominent were the history and philosophy titles.

"Dementia," Manick said, folding himself into the chair. "Mother's condition is getting worse."

"When did it start?" Shelley settled on the bed.

"Right after we moved to Dhaka."

Maya brought a tray of tea and biscuits. A woolen Kashmiri shawl hung like wings from her shoulders. She said, before leaving, that she would be found on the rooftop.

Shelley nibbled a biscuit.

"Oh," Manick said and rose. He grabbed a paperback from his desk. "I bought a Hermann Hesse novel for you."

Shelley took it and glanced at the title. *Siddhartha*. "Thank you," he said.

Manick lifted his cup and dunked a biscuit in his tea. "What are you doing tomorrow afternoon?"

"Why?"

Manick said there would be a rally at Victoria Park. A protest against the Agartala Conspiracy Case. Fears were already swelling over the success of the rally. NSF goondas were likely to ruin it. NSF was a student political organization. Backed by the government, its members' primary job was to bulldoze other student bodies and to terrorize general students so they didn't dare to speak out against the government.

"I must attend," said Shelley.

4

With bamboo batons in hands, the police were positioned along the boundary wall of Victoria Park. Yet the roaring voices from inside the park heated the chilly afternoon air outside.

"There they are," Manick said to Shelley as they arrived at the park entrance.

At that instant two NSF boys blocked their path.

"Go home, boys," one said. He had a toothpick hanging between his teeth.

"We've come to attend the meeting," Manick said.

"Meeting? What meeting? It'll be over in ten minutes. The police are set to break it down."

"Whatever. We want to get in." Shelley took a step forward.

"You motherchod!" another NSF boy yelled, pushing Shelley back hard.

"Hey, shut your dirty mouth!" Manick said.

"Ooh. You've got balls, kid," said the one holding a toothpick in his mouth. His thumb and forefinger reached for a button on Manick's shirt and started to play with it. "My hands are even dirtier. I'll cut off your balls and make you wear them as earrings. How does that sound?"

Manick slapped the hand away.

Then came the sounds of cries: *Him! NSF! Down with him!* From nowhere some activists of the Student Union showed up to help. The two NSF boys ran away at a sprint. The one with the toothpick shouted back at Manick, "We'll get you, motherchod!"

That was when Shelley recognized the notorious NSF thug known as KK. One day, not long ago, he had seen KK beating a student in Dhaka Hall, calling the victim "you motherchod!" Shelley clenched his jaw. No one ever dared to call him a motherfucker.

Inside, Victoria Park was swarming with people. Buzzing heads were all around the cenotaph. Placards jostled in the air. Onstage, a student organization leader was speaking.

"You know they don't want us to speak in Bengali. Tagore's songs are banned on radio and television. They're trying to Urdu-ize our language. Our culture. Our music."

The speaker reminded the audience about the 1954 election. The Muslim League party had thought they would be the winners. Why? Because they had the word *Muslim* attached to the party name. "But people did not vote for them. They voted for the Awami League. People proved the West Wing cannot use religion as opium anymore. Here in Bengal, Hindu and Muslims are all brothers. Bangla is our pride."

"Hindu, Muslims are brothers! Bangla is our pride!" the crowd chorused.

"The East Wing has sacrificed enough. We have a larger population than the West Wing. But with our money they set up industries there, make developments there. And in return they ignore our needs. Bengalis won't allow this discrimination anymore.

"The six-point demand is the demand for our rights. Since 1947 we've seen enough. Now it's time to stand up. You know our leaders are kept in jail on false accusations. The Agartala Conspiracy Case is nothing but a silly joke. It's a tamasha with Bengalis. Tamasha and natak, pure and simple. They have to stop all this nonsense outright. They have to release all our political prisoners."

"Release all political prisoners!" the crowd buzzed.

In every direction Shelley saw his university friends. And there was the boy, King Siraj.

"Hello, stranger!" Asad embraced Shelley.

"Hey, bro!" Fourqan shook his hand. "Welcome home. You need to be active to make the six-point movement successful. Look at me. Forever single. Forever in love. Forever hassle-free life."

Fourqan taught at a college nearby. He was having an affair with a married woman whose husband worked in the ministry.

"I've m-missed you, Shelley sir," said King Siraj.

"I am back, comrades," Shelley said with a smile. "I'll be a regular bird at the protests from today."

When Maulana Aabdar Khan rose to give a speech, the park seemed to hum. Policemen closed in. Up until now they had stayed outside, but this time they headed for the stage. The audience muttered. Holding the microphone, the maulana waited. Then with the flat of his hand he signaled to the audience to keep calm. One mustached police officer approached him, while the others positioned themselves by the stage to remind the audience of their presence.

Shelley heard some broken words. The rally could not continue. An argument broke out between the officer and the speakers. The student leader who had spoken first raised his voice. "We will not leave this place. The rally will be continued."

The murmur in the crowd grew louder. A number of them had already gathered around the altar. King Siraj started to climb the steps. Shelley caught Manick's eye. Were the pesky police going to leap onto the crowds? Fire tear gas to disperse them?

"Let me handle this, trust me," hollered the maulana to his fellow speakers. Then he faced the officer.

"We will finish it here," he suggested. "Let me just perform a dua prayer."

The officer hesitated.

The maulana stepped up with the microphone. He looked out at the audience in silence. Almost everyone was standing. A fight was likely to erupt at any moment. Without any introduction, the maulana announced, "Dear brothers, let's make a dua prayer."

The maulana raised his cupped hands in front of his face. "Ya Allah, we all have gathered here for our country, for the betterment of our nation. Please make our effort successful."

Amen! Amen! Cupping their hands in the same way, the crowd chanted with the maulana. The mustached police officer joined in the prayer, too.

"Ya Allah, the East Wing is experiencing oppression and discrimination by the West Wing rulers. They treat us like the sons of a lesser god. Allah, make their hearts kind, so that there will be no imbalance between the east and the west."

"Amen! Amen!"

The maulana was a simple man. He wore a white kurta and lungi. He had a large beard, and on his head was a straw topi hat. Some said he was a communist. Once, Shelley had asked him about it in private. The maulana replied with a serene smile that he had never read Marx or Lenin; he had come to politics to speak for the downtrodden masses.

Another time, Shelley asked him a tricky question. "What is more important, language or religion?"

The maulana narrowed his eyes, thought for ten seconds, and then said, "Both is important, but I think language has greater importance in our lives than religion."

"Why?"

"Because it's the necessity. And language is present. Religion is future. We live in the present, not in the future."

At Victoria Park, the simple maulana turned out to be shrewd. He changed everything with his magical dua prayer. It was more than a speech. He smartly delivered his best speech by seeking God's grace.

By the time the officer realized the dua prayer trap, it was too late. There was no way out then. He gnashed his teeth, glaring at the maulana.

The maulana went on to discuss the Agartala Conspiracy Case. Who was the law for? he asked. Law was for the rulers. If the police wanted to, they could put Bengalis in prison for months and months. God should look at these political prisoners. Hundreds of frivolous lawsuits were always ready to put them away, out of political life, send them to jail. If freed on one charge, they would charge them with something else. They set them free at the prison gates, then arrested them a minute later. It was a cat-and-mouse game. Why was God blind to this injustice?

"Amen! Amen! Amen!" The roaring harmony got louder and louder in the air.

CHAPTER SEVEN

1

Durga Puja festival had begun. On his way back from the *Cinemagazine* office, Shelley stopped into a local temple. The air inside the premises was alive with the fresh fragrance of incense, sweet and solid. Devotional songs were being played. There was a cluster of devotees around the marquee mandap.

The deity was in a cream silk sari with a red border, with lush, wavy black hair cascading over both shoulders. Her medium-sized lips—lustrously reddened—wore a Mona Lisa smile. Riding a tiger, the Goddess, mother of the universe, was holding a variety of weapons in her ten arms.

Shelley stood staring at the idol. There was something, something in the face of the idol that stunned him. A ripple of vibration went through his body. The deity, he figured, had the face of Roxana. Though her eyes were too large, and lips too roundish for Roxana, overall, the idol, much like Roxana, had the perfect round face and chubby cheeks. He pondered that it had been a month already.

How long Shelley stood before the idol he didn't know. His meditation soon broke from the stream of nudging and jostling visitors. His eyes became misty. How had the idol maker gotten the contours of Roxana's face? Shelley wondered. He must find the sculptor.

He inquired with the festival committee.

—

The area along the river in Rayer Bazaar was called Palpara, abounding with a plethora of pottery shops. The sculptor had a roadside shop-cum-studio. The shop sign read "Ajay Pal & Sons." At the front of his place dozens of small-sized Ganesh and Krishna idols were on display. The back space—the studio—was crowded with a couple of Kali idols in progress, along with hay, bamboo sticks, earth clay, and so forth. A nice smell of dried straw permeated the place. Shelley noticed the remnants of a Durga idol in a corner. The idol was without a head, and three out of her ten arms were missing.

Ajay Pal, a man in his forties, was in his undershirt and lungi. Shelley greeted him and asked about the Durga idol in the temple. "I'm wondering," he said, "was there any model for it?"

"Model?"

"I mean, did you sculpt the face using any model, or with someone in mind?"

"Oh, no. It's purely from my imagination."

Shelley shot him a steady look. He took a breath. "Can you make one idol—a statue basically—with the same face?"

"You want a statue?"

Shelley nodded.

"Do you have a picture of the face you want me to make?"

Shelley fished out a photo from his shirt pocket, a single photo of Roxana taken in a studio.

Ajay Pal studied it. "Yes, I can do that." He then asked about the height and other factors about the statue.

"How much would it cost?" Shelley asked.

The amount Ajay Pal quoted was three months of Shelley's income. He scratched his temple. "Look," he said, "you don't have to make it like an idol. Just make a statue of a woman. An ordinary woman. And make the face like this photograph. That's all I want. The face."

Ajay Pal bit his lips, looked up and thought.

"There's no rush," Shelley said. "You can deliver it anytime. After Kali Puja, of course."

The man cut the amount in half. Shelley calculated in his mind. He would have to borrow some money from Manick. He haggled a bit and agreed upon a reasonable figure with Ajay Pal.

"How long will it take to make?"

"Two weeks at least."

"That's fine. So when do you start?"

"You can come see me after the Kali festival."

"In the last week of October?"

"That's right. And you have to pay half the amount in advance."

"Okay, I will see you soon."

2

On Friday evening Maya said she would like to go for a walk in Ramna Park during the weekend, to have some fresh air in the green. Manick suggested that Shelley and Maya go without him; he was busy writing a paper.

The following afternoon, as the rickshaw started rolling from Dream Garden, Shelley held his breath. This was the first time he had sat so close to Maya, together in the womb of one rickshaw. He could smell her hair, her body odor. Maya was in a lavender-pink kameez and a pearl-white salwar.

"It's hot outside," Maya said, crushing the silence.

"It'll be cooler in the park," he said.

At the park entrance, Maya pointed at the street snack vendor. "Is that phoochka?"

"Yes, would you like to have some?" he said.

"I'd love to."

Shelley ordered two plates of phoochkas. They stood under the shade of a rain tree to wait.

"Rashid and I always ate phoochka when we went out," she said, as though to herself.

Shelley said nothing, his eyes on the vendor preparing the plates of phoochka. A silent sigh escaped him.

The vendor came with the plates. They ate silently. He gazed at her moving fingers.

A sweet-scented breeze swept through the place.

Maya sniffed the air. "Lovely smell. What flower is it?"

"Kadam, I suspect."

Shelley paid the vendor. They entered the park and walked side by side. He noticed her underarms, clammy with sweat.

"I used to come here with Father when he was alive, for afternoon walks," Maya said.

"Since then you haven't been here?"

"No. It's been . . . two years and nine months."

"It's a nice park. A green heaven in Dhaka. When I feel really down, I come here."

"And you walk and walk?"

"Sometimes I lie on the grass and watch the sky."

Maya halted and turned to him. "You're a poet at heart."

"I don't know. I do at times dabble in poetry, yes."

"I liked a few of your poems, though."

Shelley said nothing. He hadn't written anything since Roxana's death. He planted a cigarette between his lips, lit it, and began to smoke.

"Earlier you never smoked before me. Now you don't bother."

"Oh, I'm sorry. Do you . . . mind?"

"I do, and I don't. But it's all right." Maya half raised her hand.

They slow-walked along the lake in silence. Some unknown birds were chattering in the trees.

"Can I have a drag on your cigarette?"

Shelley stopped. "Are you serious?"

Maya said she'd once tried it many years ago. Her friend Deepika had stolen a cigarette from her brother. "It was an awful experience," she laughed.

He began to grab a fresh cigarette, but she wanted the one he was smoking. Her cheeks swelled from taking two short puffs, and a second later she started coughing. She returned the cigarette. "I don't know what people find in this crap."

Shelley laughed and glanced at the smudge of her lipstick on the cigarette end. He took a long drag and thought about the evening Roxana had tried smoking.

"I didn't tell you," Shelley said. "Something strange happened last week. A small serendipity." He told her about his visit to the temple— the Durga idol's facial resemblance to Roxana.

"How's that possible?" Maya said.

"I talked to the idol maker. He said he made it completely out of his imagination."

"Are you sure he never saw your wife?"

"No way."

"Strange!" Maya broke off. "Let's sit here on the grass."

They sat. A boy was hawking roasted peanuts nearby. Shelley bought some.

"Can I ask you something?" Maya said, cracking a peanut.

Shelley nodded.

"Roxana. Was she beautiful?"

Shelley observed a crop of sparring sparrows for a few seconds. He sighed and said, "She was."

"Do you have her photo?"

"I have. But not with me in my wallet." Shelley glanced at Maya. Her hair was over her face. Her eyes down on her fingers. She was picking at her nails. "You should stop biting your nails," he said.

Her fingers came to rest. "Why?"

"They look lousy."

She spread out her fingers. All gnawed down and bloody looking.

"See what you've done."

"Let's walk," Maya said after a while.

They rose and walked through the trees.

—

Before their rickshaw left for home from behind the central mosque, a gentle drizzle began to fall. Shelley eyed Maya watching the street. The shops. Smoke from the grilling seekh kebabs at a restaurant. A passing bullock cart. A roaring Volkswagen. She hummed a tune to herself.

"Ehe, you're much darker than me," she said, indicating Shelley's left arm, which had slightly touched her right arm.

Shelley rolled his sleeve to the elbow. He studied her arm to compare their skin color. His arm was sturdy, thinly covered with soft brown hair. Hers was slim, hairless, and fairer than his.

The drizzle turned to light rain now. Shelley pulled the rickshaw hood forward to cover their heads from the rain. "Your hair smells of jasmine," he said.

"I use jasmine oil."

He stole a quick glance at her. The rickshaw rolled onto Narinda Road.

"That's a great place to visit." Shelley pointed out the Christian Cemetery across the road.

"Are you a necropolis lover?"

"Well . . . I like this place for its silence and serenity."

"But it's a burial ground."

"I think what appeals to me is auld lang syne. Many British and Europeans were buried here. I wonder about those foreigners. Thousands of miles away from their families and countries of birth. Some tombs are pretty old. Good for historical knowledge."

Maya glanced at him. "Do you pray sometimes?"

"Do I pray? No. I'm not a believer."

"You don't believe in God?"

He shook his head lightly. "I don't see any use anyway. God rather makes me confused."

"Really?" She gave him a hard look.

He shrugged.

She watched the receding rain in silence.

At Dream Garden the rickshaw pulled in. Shelley paid the fare while Maya rapped on the front gate. The gate opened, and she walked in ahead of him. By the living room, she stopped and turned to Shelley.

"My head hurts. I need a nap. You could stay or leave." She started for her room without waiting for an answer.

3

On Wednesday afternoon, Shelley pulled out a paperback from his satchel and held it out to Maya. "I want you to read this book."

Maya put her teacup down and took it. She eyed the cover—a meditating Buddha statue with a black background. "*Siddhartha*," she read the title.

"Yes, a novel. I finished it last week."

"A novel? I can't read novels anymore. Don't have that much patience."

"Go slow," he said. "Take your time. It's a good one."

"*Good, bad* . . . these words have long lost their charm on me." Maya flicked her hair off her eye. She laid the paperback on the tea table.

He rubbed his chin. "Buddhism makes life simple."

"Is it about Buddha?"

"Yes . . . no. It's about spirituality. Happiness."

"You know what, when I first read about Buddha in school, I didn't like him."

"Strange. Why?"

"Because he left his wife and child. What kind of husband and father was he? So irresponsible!"

"He did it to find the bigger meaning in life."

"Doesn't matter. He didn't care about them. That's the point."

"Well, he left them in good care. His father was a king."

"So what?" she said. "It was Buddha who was needed as a husband and father. A grandfather cannot do that job. Buddha is still an irresponsible person to me."

"Look—"

"I know what you're trying to say. Just stop it."

Shelley fell silent, astonished by her tone.

"I'm a believer. I've inherited a religion from my parents. That's enough for me." Maya crossed her arms and leaned back on the sofa. A minute later, eyes keeping on the floor, she said, "I'm sorry."

He nodded with a strained smile.

"You know, when I got sick, my father encouraged me to pray. He said prayer was the best medicine for our souls. We can forget God, but God never forgets us." She paused. "Maybe I should start praying again."

Shelley said nothing.

"Do I sound like a mad girl to you?"

"Nah. Not in the least."

She sneered. "Madness runs under the skin of our family."

"Was there anyone in your extended family?"

"My maternal uncle," she sighed.

She told him her uncle's story. She had been a teenager then. It all started one winter. Maya's uncle awoke one night and commanded his wife to get out of bed. When she asked the reason, without warning he started to pee on the blanket. Screaming, his wife leaped to her feet. That was the beginning. Until he stepped into the grave, every winter he turned completely mad. Dashed out into the street with nothing on. Once Maya encountered her uncle running naked.

"That doesn't prove anything," Shelley said.

"I will go mad. I can feel it. Some days I feel shut down. Some days I feel a heat inside me. That drives me nuts."

"We all are mad, in some way."

"Almost everyone feels better over time," Maya said after a while.

"You mean me?" Shelley sensed her hint.

"Yeah. You're back to school. Back to your friends, addas, and protests. All over again."

"That's life, Maya."

"That's life, that's life," she exploded. "Don't you ever tell me that. I'm sick of hearing that hogwash. I don't want to be what you all want me to be. I'm fine as I am."

4

It was Friday. After leaving the office in the late afternoon, Shelley figured he had nothing to do. He thought of going to Madhur Canteen. He walked toward Nawabpur Road. Near the stadium, loitering post-rally attendees from Paltan Maidan pushed past him. He spotted King Siraj eating chickpeas on the side of the street. He tapped the boy's back.

The boy swung round. "Shelley sir! Were you in the rally? I d-d-didn't see you."

"No, I'm coming from work."

"Asad sir, Fourqan sir—a-a-all were there. They're off to university now."

"Don't worry. I'll catch up with them."

They walked. Shoving the last bits of chickpeas into his mouth, King Siraj released the paper container into the street.

"Shelley sir? Isn't your office near Victoria Park?"

"That's right."

"Sir, I heard your wife's dead. Is it true?"

Shelley gave a slight nod.

"How, sir? She was sooo beautiful." The boy had met Roxana just once.

"Let's not talk about it," Shelley suggested.

The boy kept quiet.

"Have you visited your mother recently?"

King Siraj ignored the question. "Bitch," he mumbled.

"Where does she live now?"

"Malibagh slum." He sprayed saliva through his teeth. "The whore married again. Third time."

"It's okay. You shouldn't call your mother a whore." Shelley paused. "What does this husband do?"

"Mugging." The boy strutted, looking across the street at the Secretariat building. His feet were bare as always.

King Siraj continued talking. The week before he had broken the nose of that mugger. He went to see his mother upon request one afternoon. The mugger was home. King Siraj sat at the edge of the small bed. His scraggy mother, after marriage, seemed to have grown a wee bit stout.

"Are you pregnant?" he asked plainly.

His mother did not answer.

"Yeah," answered the mugger, laughing. His mouth, when he talked, drizzled tiny droplets of saliva. His sunken cheeks and eyes looked haggard.

His mother touched King Siraj's long hair and told him he should get a haircut. She asked this and that.

"Whassyourname? Siraijja? Siraijja? Huh?" The mugger spoke. "Go get cigarettes for me." In his extended hand was a coin.

King Siraj kept silent.

"Hey? Siraijja? You deaf? Go. The shop's over there."

"I'm not your servant."

"Of course, you're my servant. Who the fuck are you then? President?" The mugger began to curse Siraj and yell at his mother.

King Siraj knew very little about his father, his mother's first husband. A vegetable vendor. Not a bad person, but he was paranoid and used to beat her for no reason. "Haramzadi, why does the man next door stare at you?" Or "Chootmarani, why did that shortarse smile at you?" "Khankimagi, why does your booty sway when you walk?" That was it. He needed no excuse to whack her. He did it to make her a well-behaved wife.

Mother's bruised skin was used to regular beatings, but her untamed voice screamed loud. Years later, once in a while, still King Siraj would hear her screaming in his sleep.

The vegetable seller, returning home early one day, took to his bed. And in less than a week, he died of malaria. Mother then married a rickshawwallah, who had another wife. This man treated her well. He came to sleep with her two to three times a week, but barely paid the family expenses. So she took a maidservant job and left him. King Siraj and his mother moved to the master's house and stayed in the kitchen at night.

On a certain night as the boy tried to touch his mother in sleep, he felt a man's fatty, fleshy body. Ma? he cried in fear. Shhh, Mother hissed.

"Don't you ever wake up crying at night," his mother threatened him the next morning.

"I was scared."

"Nothing to be scared of. You must've had a bad dream."

A few months later there was a quarrel in the house. The householder and his wife were yelling at each other. Then, before dusk, the wife had Mother and King Siraj leave the house.

"Where shall we go now?" King Siraj asked his mother out in the street.

She slapped him on both cheeks. "It's you. It all happened because of you."

The little boy couldn't fathom how he was responsible for this. Had he cried out in his sleep while having bad dreams?

Night fell. They slept in a park. In the morning they strayed about the storehouses by the river. It worked. Within days Mother found various jobs there. Sweeping, cleaning, washing vegetables. On and off, working as a coolie at the Buriganga River port, Siraj could also earn a little. Occasionally he would go to Sutrapur to push rickshaws up the bridge. The coins he earned got him a cheap snack.

Weeks went by. He learned to survive on his own, distancing himself from his mother. On a rain-soaked night, he was asleep at a station.

A creepy sensation on his neck awakened him. He sat right up to find a centipede brushing past him. What if it had sneaked into his ear? That was how they got inside your head and ate the brains, he'd heard. The fright was so intense that he longed to sleep beside his mother, holding her tight.

Now, with the vague memory of his vegetable vendor father, something sprang up in King Siraj. "Don't you talk dirty about my father," he said to the mugger.

The mugger cackled with delight. He said that both King Siraj and his vegetable vendor father were bastards. He said he could absolutely guarantee it.

King Siraj did not wait to ask how the mugger could prove this. Without warning he punched the mugger in the jaw and took to his heels.

5

From Madhur Canteen, just before nine, Shelley and Manick headed for home. They found a rickshaw near the library. Shelley fished out his pack of Capstan from his pocket and offered Manick a cigarette.

"How's Maya doing?" he asked Manick.

Manick didn't speak for a few seconds. "She tried to cut her mole."

"What? Why?"

"Why don't you ask her yourself?" Manick sighed. After a silence he said, "Do you know why our family moved to Dhaka from Kolkata?"

Shelley looked at his face but said nothing.

"We moved to Dhaka solely for Maya. Father thought she'd have a fresh life and forget her past wounds. But—" He paused and sighed. "I don't know, I'm still hoping to see his words come true. I really am."

There was a long pause.

"She's been down in the dumps lately," Manick said. "Her sleepless-ness is back. Now for two days she's been murmuring to herself."

Murmuring to herself? Shelley looked at him in disbelief.

It all started, Manick went on, after Rashid's disappearance, after the riots. Maya turned terribly quiet. They supposed she'd be all right. Just a matter of time. But she stopped speaking, sleeping. Eating, too. She began talking to herself. They transferred her to the IOP hospital in Kolkata. She improved. The doctors advised them not to push her about anything. All she needed was support and company. "We do our best, you know," he sighed, "but depression's killing her."

"Have you spoken to her doctor here?"

"Her doctor's out of town." Manick said. "The stupid thing is there's no psychiatric service in Dhaka."

"Nothing at all?"

"Almost nothing. Don't even mention that loony bin in Pabna."

Pabna Medical Hospital, the only psychiatric institute in the East Province, was located in another district. Manick was right. As far as Shelley knew, that place belonged to people with severe mental illness.

"There's nothing here," Manick insisted.

The tone of his voice was gruff and unforgiving. His frustration was clear. The frustration of moving from a big city to a small city. The frustration of leaving behind a big country. Kolkata had become the first capital of the British Raj in the late eighteenth century. Dhaka on the other hand had become important only after Partition.

—

The following evening Shelley went to Dream Garden. When Manick brought Maya to the living room and sat her down, Shelley noticed that her face looked gaunt, her hair undone. The Marilyn Monroe beauty spot had her left cheek inflamed, reddened, leaving a bad scar.

Shelley greeted her. Maya did not respond, did not blink. She was nonchalant.

"Maya!" Manick touched her arm. She slightly turned her head, staring at Shelley.

"Shelley, have you told Maya about your Banglish professor?" Manick winked.

No, Shelley had not. He began his account in the hope of making her smile. The Banglish professor had an oriental body in an occidental costume. All year round he dressed in a three-piece suit. But how did he cope with the sultry Bengal air? a student once asked him. Inside him, he replied, he breathed English air. Even at the dinner table, when at home, he maintained this natty attire.

The Banglish professor was tall and had a perfectly accented English tongue. He was more British than the British. Only one thing— his brown skin—betrayed him. He regretted this. The Banglish professor delighted in teaching English manners. Too often he encouraged or forced the students to wear formal dress. It would civilize the nation, he believed. He favored Shelley, though. "I like your name," he would say whenever Shelley bumped into him.

"Here comes the fun part," Shelley said, checking on Maya. The same professor had lately started wearing sherwani and a Jinnah cap. He had totally stopped speaking Bangla. There was gossip in the wind that he was going to be the next vice chancellor of the university. As a matter of fact, now he wanted to come across as a perfect Pakistani. But this getup made him look like a clown. He would have looked even better if he'd started wearing pantaloons.

Maya stood up in a huff. "Why are you telling me this nonsense?" She walked out.

—

During dinner Manick doubted the government would withdraw the Agartala Conspiracy Case. People were going crazy. The military ought to understand that "beefy hands with vapid heads" did not work. The "left-right parade brainpower" was good for using a gun, but not for running a country. Field Marshal Ayub Khan had pretty much proved it.

Shelley half listened. His plate was replete with pulao rice, fish fry, chicken curry, and salad. They smelled delicious, but he had no appetite. A question was bubbling in his mind: Had Maya eaten?

CHAPTER EIGHT

1

On a crisp November evening Shelley brought Roxana home from the idol maker. He placed her next to his bed. She was swathed in outdated newspaper. He unwrapped her, dropping her covers one by one. Shelley ceased as his hand reached to strip her from waist down. He looked at her large stony eyes, which seemed to be saying, "Don't be greedy."

When he had been at Ajay Pal's studio that afternoon, he felt awkward. He was uncomfortable about checking the naked statue of Roxana in the presence of the idol maker. He felt that he was humiliating Roxana by keeping her unclothed in front of a stranger. "It's perfect," he told the idol maker. "Please wrap her up with something."

Now Roxana was home. Shelley removed the last newspaper covering, pegged a cigarette between his fingers, and stood before Roxana to study every inch of her body. Three feet in height, the figure was plump, unlike Roxana. Which was okay with him. All he'd asked the sculptor to do was focus on the face—the eyes, lips, chin.

The eyes were a little big, cheeks chubbier, and chin wider, but overall, it was the face of Roxana. The breasts were ravishingly round and full. Soft curves around the stomach. The belly button deep. Waist amply wide, thighs pudgy, her legs were apart with weight on the left foot.

No matter how Shelley stared and stared and went on staring, Roxana outstared him every time. And he had to glance away for a second from her powerful eyes that didn't blink. He tenderly touched her face. The tip of his finger almost floated on the valley of her upper lip, as if his touch might mar her delicacy.

In the space of half an hour, lying in bed, Shelley finished three cigarettes. His eyes were fixed on Roxana. There was an overwhelming power of seduction in a nude statue, he thought, the au naturel figure hypnotizing the watcher like an invisible gravitational pull.

He didn't know when he nodded off. When he sensed a soft touch on his foot, he fluttered his eyes open to a soft, quasi-inaudible voice: *Hey! Hey!* He found Roxana looking at him, smiling sweetly.

Shelley peered at Roxana's statue without breathing. She was hardly a hand away from the head of his bed, where he'd placed her. The front of her was facing in the direction of his head. He extended his hand and touched her hip.

"Roxana! Roxana!" he said. "Did you just speak?"

There was no response. No stirring from Roxana.

"Please, Roxana! I know you spoke. I just heard you."

Shelley threw his feet on the floor, grabbed the ill-lit hurricane lamp from the desk, and held it near Roxana's face. He stared at her for a long moment. "You ought to wear something," he mumbled.

He dug out the bag where he still kept Roxana's clothes and took out a sari. He tied one end of the sari in a knot wrapping around her waist, below the belly button. He wrapped it two times around, tucking the upper end into the loop. Then he draped the end portion of the sari over her left shoulder.

He took a step back to survey her novel looks. Not immaculate. The dress looked like a long piece of fabric badly wrapped around her body. What was missing were the pleats, he figured.

"I'm sorry, dear. Tomorrow I will check how women wear it."

2

After class was over, on James Joyce's *Ulysses*, Shelley parked himself in Madhur Canteen. He spotted a knot of crowd cluster around their regular table. Asad's voice was loud. Manick was sitting still, long ash on his cigarette, a pucker between his eyebrows.

"I won't leave the dorm," Asad said. "I'll take it to the end."

"Look," said Fourqan. "We're not asking you to retreat like a chicken. Just be safe for a while."

"What happened?" To Shelley's inquiring no one said boo. He tapped the person next to him. "Hey Babool, what's the matter?"

"Where were you, man? Your friends have been attacked."

Shelley drew him to one side. "I was in class. What happened?"

"KK kicked their asses."

"You're kidding me. Why?"

"What do you mean why? Do the NSF bastards need any *why* to beat somebody?"

Heat pooled in Shelley's voice. "Ah, tell me everything."

"KK lives in the same dorm Asad does. You probably know that?"

"Of course."

Babool began from the beginning. That morning Asad and Manick were having tea at the canteen. Manick had no classes till noon. Asad asked him to accompany him to his residence hall for protest poster writing. Manick complied.

At the front gate of the dorm, KK was smoking. The moment Asad and Manick walked by, KK summoned them, asking the reason why they had passed him without any greeting. "Is this what you learn at the Oxford of the East?" KK yelled in their face, telling them to say sorry and salaam him. But Asad, an active Student Union worker, walked away, pulling Manick's arm.

Barely ten minutes zipped by before KK and his gang stormed into Asad's room with hockey sticks. They smashed up everything. Tables, books, clothes, mattresses—everything. Panicked, Asad and Manick watched the whole thing without uttering a word. The worst part was KK then had them peel off their clothes. When they refused to remove their pants, he cut the clothing with a razor. Then he paraded them on the balcony like circus clowns, only in their underwear.

"No one, no one came for help?" Shelley was taken aback. His face hardened.

"Help? Who would fight the NSF? They had hockey sticks, knives, razors. Arms as well." Babool reckoned some of the students would have gathered to chase the bastards away, but most were out in classes. The few who happened to be in the dorm at the time didn't have the guts to take on the NSF.

"Did the bastards beat them up?"

"No. But taking off your clothes is worse than being beaten up, isn't it?" Babool said. "It could have been a lot worse, though. What if KK had locked them in the room and released his cobra?"

Everyone knew that KK had a pet cobra. Shelley shivered, imagining a slithering snake in a locked room.

—

Later when their table was free from visitors, the four friends were alone. Manick and Asad looked odd in their borrowed clothes. Manick's shirt was too tight, Asad's pants too ample.

"I think," said Manick, "KK remembered my face and wanted to shame Asad in front of me. To show his muscle."

"Forget it. What about a written complaint?" suggested Shelley.

"To whom?" Fourqan said.

"To the hall provost."

"Where on earth do you live? NSF boys are backed by the governor. You'd never get fair judgment."

"It's Professor Rahman who is in charge. Very strict provost."

"So?" Manick shot a raging glance at Shelley. "Governor Monem Khan will telephone to tell him not to take action against his boys. Excuse them this time. End of story."

Asad pulled hard at his Che mustache. "See these two arms? I've done enough fighting in my life. If . . . if I had been alone, for heaven's sake there would have been a murder today. Either KK or me, one of us would be dead." His hand curled into a fist.

"We know your type," Fourqan said. "What's your plan now, anyway?"

"I'm moving to a friend's place," Asad said. "But I'll get my revenge."

3

The next day, around noon, KK blew into the canteen.

The second Shelley saw KK, he kicked Manick under the table. Manick's back was to the gate that KK had come through, and Asad also sat across the table opposite Shelley. By the time Manick gave Shelley a *what-is-it* face, KK stood right behind Shelley. His three companions ringed the table, just like in Western movies, all in big sunglasses with long hair and longish sideburns, as if ready for a shoot-out.

Voices, smoke, and the noise of the canteen came to a halt.

"Hey, boys," cracked the voice of KK above Shelley. "How's it going?"

Asad looked at KK, outraged.

"The country requires good guys like me to shut you up," KK said. "You hear?" The toothpick in his mouth made his voice sluggish.

Shelley watched Manick and Asad glance up above his head. He could sense that the eyes of the whole canteen were on their table.

KK's forefinger swooped down for a carpenter ant on the table's edge. It had been eating a bread crumb. His finger kept squashing the ant's abdomen, while the ant wildly squirmed right and left to be free.

"This is how we teach the naughty ones." His finger withdrew. Squashed, the ant's abdomen was broken off. It struggled to shift its half-gone body.

KK turned and strode out. His folks followed him.

Once KK left, visitors from neighboring tables huddled around them. They said they had all been poised to strike had KK dared to touch a single hair of Asad or Manick's head. Who did the NSF boys think they were? The doomsday of the NSF dogs was close. Student organization workers said there was nothing to be afraid of. We are with you, they confirmed.

"It'll be a tit-for-tat game," Asad told Manick afterward to cheer him up. "I know a gang from Kandupatti ghetto. Already talked to them. Any further attack comes upon you or me, will be doubly returned."

Manick was sullen, silent.

"Why do you think KK is after us?" asked Shelley.

"To terrorize us," Asad said. "And through us to terrorize other students who are getting active in the six-point movement."

"All sensible students are up for this movement. How many will they go after?"

"Until all sensible students grow the urge to stand against them."

Manick snorted.

Asad looked at Manick. "That'll happen pretty soon. A bunch of NSF bastards can't strangle every student's voice."

—

At two in the afternoon Shelley was near Sharif Mia's Canteen, waiting for a rickshaw, when King Siraj popped up before him. He was wearing a grimy undershirt, holes here and there, and khaki shorts that turned out to be full pants for him.

"Shelley sir, you're leaving to work?"

"Yeah. What's up?"

"Can I ask you something?"

"What is it?"

The boy asked if it was true that KK had beat up Asad and Manick and made them walk naked. Shelley took a breath. "All a pack of lies. Their pants were cut off with a razor. Nothing more."

King Siraj listened, then did a calculation in his mind. "Sir, will you buy me a good kn-n-nife?"

"Knife? What for?"

"I will kill KK."

Shelley touched the boy's cheek tenderly. "You little fool."

"I am se-erious. Killing is easy. I will s-s-stab and run."

"What do you think the police do? Suck lollipops? They'll catch you."

"Nah. They're all fat. I can o-o-outpace them," King Siraj said. If, unfortunately, he got caught, he reckoned, jail was not that bad. Free food and a roof to sleep under sounded fine to him. He'd heard no one aged below eighteen was executed. So there was nothing to fear.

4

Manick didn't talk much about that dorm incident. Shelley didn't ask about it, either. But that nightmare was still hovering around Manick. The disgrace was killing him. Shelley could see it in Manick's eyes.

They were sipping Darjeeling tea in the living room, and soon they ran out of conversation. Maya suggested they go to the rooftop. Manick seemed clearly relieved, asking Maya to take Shelley.

Maya carried her tea along. She was in a banana-leaf-green sari that reflected the afternoon light. She'd gotten over her dark mood recently and looked fine. Half the roof was stroked by the sun. Sunlight slipped down Maya's untied hair.

"Manick," she said, looking at the crown of the coconut tree. "What's gotten into him? Something must be bothering him."

Shelley crossed his arms and thought for a second. "Just let it go. Nothing significant you should know of."

She sighed. "How's your study going?"

"It's okay."

"You been busy lately?"

"A bit."

"A bit?" she repeated.

"Well, had some extra work at the office. Plus private tutoring. My own study. University. You know."

"Hmm, I know. People change with time. Only I can't." After a short silence, she spoke. Her eyes shone. "Can you take me to protest marches and demonstrations? I want to shout at the top of my lungs. Punch the air with an angry fist."

Shelley laughed. "Yes, I can. But it's not safe anymore. Police are getting violent and awfully crazy." He thought of something. "You can help us in another way. How's your handwriting?"

"Not too bad."

"Then you can write posters for us. I'll talk to Manick."

She ambled along the railing, ceased gazing down on the street. Then she bent over the flower tubs and shook a drying-up red rose. A few petals fell off.

"Being alive is like being in a war every day," she said, straightening up, her face utterly strange. "I'm tired of living."

Shelley eyed her in silence.

A moment later, without warning, it started to rain hard in big drops. But the sky was clear and cloudless.

"Get in here." Maya dashed into the attic.

He followed.

The stuffy attic smelled sour, dampish. Shabby old furniture, moldering mattress, a lidless tin trunk, shoes, sacks, and bags—all were mixed up in heaps, choking up the corner and the only window. For some time they listened to the pattering of raindrops on the corrugated iron roof. They breathed in the scent of the fresh rain mingled with dust. It was the untimely rain heralding the winter.

"You know what," she said, "I feel guilty being alive. Sometimes I forget I exist. Or what it feels like to be happy. Or beautiful." She paused and sighed. Then she asked how she looked today.

"You look beautiful," he said.

"I was expecting to hear it from you earlier."

Her words "from you" reverberated in his ears. "You look grand in green."

She sniggered. "My body is grand too."

Her words screeched, jumbled in his head.

"You don't believe me, right?"

He was still.

"I've been thinking over the last few days. Beauty is wasted if nobody looks at it. It's not worth keeping, then. Beauty deserves to be praised. To be worshipped. Enjoyed. Didn't you ever want to see me naked?"

Shelley couldn't speak. He wrestled to keep pace with her words.

She dropped the sari end of her shoulder.

A blouse masking two mountains flared open. He could make out her feminine beauty inside—her impossible breasts, full and firm, as delicate as a blushing bride's. She had sinewy shoulders, her skin smooth. Her glaring collarbones bold like the midrib of a banana leaf. Her bare midriff flaunting her belly button.

Shelley found no breathable air in the attic. He felt his animal growing and groaning.

"Did I ever tell you that I adore water hyacinth flowers?" her voice dripped. "Beauty is a bizarre thing. Water hyacinths are such unnecessary, unneeded, and worthless plants. No one bothers to lay eyes on them. But they have beautiful soft-purple flowers."

It was not her leaflike lips talking, he imagined, but her breathing breasts. They had the delicacy of touch-me-not plants. There was a mole, he noted, right above her cleavage. Could he touch that? What would happen, he wondered, if he jumped on her, took her in his arms? Or he could lay her on the floor and do it . . . do what a man and a woman—sick with oozing lust—should do.

"Am I not beautiful?" she said.

"Y-e-aah." He was shaking, his ears burning.

"Tell me. Tell me. Tell me. I want to believe I'm beautiful. I want to believe I'm still beautiful."

"You are beautiful."

He heard the deafening drumming of his heart. As he began to breathe rapidly and rhythmically, his hand frantically reached for her breast.

She stirred, inched backward, and the flat of her hand struck his face. A swift, sharp slap. She gave a shrill cry. "How dare you!"

Then she spun around, draped her sari end over the shoulder covering her blouse, and stormed off.

He was transfixed. The rain had stopped. By the last gleams of the dying day, her last words lingered in his ears. And inside his head, against his skull wall, her last look was engraved like a prehistoric cave painting.

5

Padding downstairs, Shelley slipped out of Dream Garden. He snaked through the serpentine Basu Bazaar Lane. At the sweet shop on Doyaganj intersection, a potbellied man, soaked in salty sweat, was frying jilapis. He stacked the crispy fried ones in a big tray. Some stray boys, along with a mangy dog, stared at it senselessly.

Loudspeakers in mosques announced the call to evening prayer. Trudging up the road, not half an hour later, he stood on the Loharpool Bridge to catch his breath. The water under the bridge was murky, and the smell of feces was flying around like an invisible bird. He turned and watched. Rickshaws, bicycles, motorcycles, handcarts, oxcarts were coming up and going down. Little boys pushed rickshaws to get rickshaw drivers across the high bridge effortlessly. The reward given by the passengers was pay-what-you-want.

"Biryani! Biryani! Sindhi biryani! The finest biryani in Pakistan! Try it once and you will remember it ever and forever!" The street biryani vendor, at one end of the bridge, shouted at the top of his sickly lungs.

Shelley started down the bridge. He sauntered through the queue for water in the street, the paan shop crowd, the gossip at tea shops; past the eating mouths of steaming seekh kebabs, the roasted-nut seller kid whose nut basket seemed heavier than him. He enjoyed the sounds of a recurring humming from a printing press, the roaring from a passing three-wheeled scooter, the swearing from a Bakarkhani roti shop.

Finally he parked himself at Beauty Boarding to have early supper. Someone he knew waved at him from a table. Shelley waved back, heading for a corner table. The waiter made an appearance, and he placed an order.

—

A dog was sitting by the garbage dump on Ghost Lane. He sat up as Shelley arrived. *Woof, woof*, he greeted him. Shelley did not reply. He carefully put some steps between the dog and pieces of torn chicken guts. He spat. The spit splattered on the wall like bird shit.

The moss-green one-room house at the end of the alley was awaiting him. The sky was clear, and the path was ablaze with silver lights. He found his room flooded by the full moon. He undressed in the moonbeam and then lit a cigarette.

Shelley didn't light up the hurricane lamp. He stood before Roxana and watched her in the soft dark. His forefinger landed on the center of her forehead, it grazed down along the ridge of her nose and parked at her upper lip. He touched her throat, felt her bare right shoulder. They were smooth, inviting. He brushed the sari drape off her left shoulder. The sari slid off her bosom. The memory of that afternoon in the attic came back to him outright. Why had Maya done it? he wondered. He fingered Roxana's cleavage. He placed his flat palm on her breast. But all he could see was Maya's open bosom. He unwrapped the sari from Roxana's waist and tossed it on the bed.

He looked over Roxana's bare statue. He put one hand on her hip and the other under her arm. He lifted her off the floor and gently pressed her against his body. He sniffed her. A fresh smell of dry clay soil filled his lungs. For a while he remained still, then his mouth began to nuzzle her ear, neck, shoulder. He put a soft kiss on her mouth. A shuddering jolted his body. He planted his mouth on her breast and sucked it hard. His breathing quickened. He held Roxana hard.

6

It was late afternoon. Shelley found Maya on the rooftop. Her mug of tea sat on the brick railing, and next to it, resting her hands, she was looking up at the sky. She was wearing a pearl-white kameez and the hem of her orna dupatta touched the ground. Her back was to the stairway, unaware of Shelley's arrival.

He savored this silent moment. Then Maya swung around abruptly. Her eyebrows raised, her lips parted, but no words came out. She turned and quickly placed her orna on her head and draped it around her neck. She went back to watching the sky and then the street. As if she were still unaware of his presence.

Shelley found her act of hair-covering very unusual but asked nothing. He cleared his throat. "Wouldn't it be nice to be together?" he said.

Maya remained unmoved.

"I mean it. Together—you and me."

She shot him a look. For two seconds their eyes met.

"Life changes. We have to roll with it."

There was a long silence before she spoke. "I've slept on it, Shelley. Given it enough thinking—about you and me. I assumed we two wounded hearts could make a fine couple. But . . ." She sighed. "Nah, we better shouldn't do it."

"What makes you think that?"

"Our indelible pasts. They're clinging to our necks like Sindbad's ghost."

"Time heals everything, Maya. Even time eats itself."

"Our scars are too big to heal, Shelley. Remember what you told me in Ramna Park? Idol Saraswati's face appeared to you as Roxana."

"So?"

"As I said, we're married to our pasts. Two more shadows will always breathe between us. How would I know when you hold me that you aren't thinking about your dead wife? How would I know if she hides in our bed at night?" She caught her breath and said, "Still . . . I still see Roxana in your eyes. You still smell of your dead wife."

There was a pause.

"And the same goes for me," she said. "How would you be sure I won't be thinking of Rashid when I touch you?"

"Nothing is wrong with that. No one can replace anyone. I'm not asking you to."

"You'll get nothing out of a neurotic girl," Maya said. "I'm all decayed."

"You're fine. It's just the depression."

"Yes, depression. And depression is contagious. That's why I want you to stay out of me."

"This is ridiculous."

Maya cocked her head. "I don't wish to hurt you. But here's the thing. I can't love you."

"I can wait, Maya."

"I tried, Shelley. Once I was jealous about your wife, of course. But since you've returned single, I've tried over and over. I thought we'd make a good couple. But I can't. I can't replace Rashid with anyone."

"I like you as you are."

She sighed. "That's sweet of you. But I can't."

He gently held her hand. Her palm was warm and soft.

"And besides—"

"Besides?"

"I can't marry an atheist."

Shelley slowly released her hand.

"I have started praying. I want to be a devout Muslim."

"That's fine. We won't hurt each other's beliefs."

"That won't work. We are on the two opposite poles when it comes to God."

"God, god, god! Religious belief!" he snapped. "India was partitioned on that stupid belief. What good has it done? This country, Pakistan, was created in favor of one religious group, and it's failing every day. You believe in God? Where was God when Rashid was killed in the riots? Where was God when they took Roxana away from me? God, god! He is as good as the dead moon in the sky. There is nothing more. It's all in our head. All illusion."

"Enough! Enough!" she yelled. "Shut your mouth, for Allah's sake! I can't hear it anymore! Who do you think you are, huh? You read a few books and you think you know everything? Everything! You wake up one day believing there is no god! You are despicable!" She looked the other way and shaded her eyes with her hand.

Shelley didn't know what to say.

Maya sniffled and wiped her tears. "Do you know why I am still alive? I'd have killed myself long ago if I didn't believe in God. My religion says suicide is the greatest sin. I don't expect much from this world. My mind, my dreams, my hopes—everything died with Rashid's death.

But I will hate you most if you try to take away the other world from me. Don't you even dare."

"I'm sorry," he said. "I didn't mean to hurt your feelings."

She exhaled. "I understand your frustration. But you're mistaken. All those things you said about religion has nothing to do with it. It's we who are creating chaos in the name of religion." There was a long pause. "I know you have a good heart. You converted to Islam. It probably means nothing to you. But Allah is kind, you know. Why don't you ask for His forgiveness and pray sometimes? Just give it a shot." She looked at him, her damp eyes pleading.

He sighed. "I genuinely wish I could. But I just can't. I can't fake it. How can I lie to my heart?" He took a glance at her. "Again, no hard feelings. My soul is hardened. And there's no room for God in there."

She stared at him for two seconds. Her eyes fluttered, and she turned around, hands holding the railing.

"Rashid," he said. "Was he religious?"

Maya gazed across the coconut leaves. "He was a believer. Like me. I was never religious. My parents never forced me into saying prayers or fasting. But I never doubted God." She turned to him. "How about Roxana?"

"She was a believer, I guess."

"You guess?"

"Well, we never found God that important to talk about."

There was silence.

She adjusted her orna over her head, covering her hair. "Can I make a request?"

Shelley looked at her. She was staring at the floor.

"Don't come to see me anymore."

"Why?"

"Because I don't want you to. Because you and your ungodly thoughts make me sick."

Shelley felt a sudden tightness in his chest, and a stabbing sadness throbbed within him. His eyes began to burn.

7

After the humiliating dorm occurrence with KK, Manick cut his canteen time. He attended classes, stepped into the library if required, and otherwise headed homeward. With final-year exams looming, he defended his absence to Shelley.

"I believe you count me as your closest friend," Shelley said, sitting in Manick's room. It must be the shame, he thought. The disgrace had gone deep. The other day he'd caught Manick coming out of a bar. Another day going into a matinee show. All by himself.

"It's killing me, Shelley," Manick opened up. "I can't take it at all. It's been all over campus. Everybody knows everything. You know Zerin in my class? She asked me about it."

Shelley knew Zerin. She was the tallest and prettiest girl in the arts faculty. When she walked by, all the eyes around walked behind her, breaking into whispers.

"I'm planning to take my master's in America."

"America?" Shelley parroted. "America?"

Manick nodded. "I'm thinking. I'm also thinking of relocating the family to Kolkata."

"You don't say."

"My cousin recently returned from London after reading for the bar exam."

"Your cousin?"

"Yes, in Kolkata," Manick said. "He's like an older brother to us. He'll be happy to take care of the family in my absence."

"What are you talking about? Are you deranged?"

"I'm talking like a sensible man. Maya can consult a good psychiatrist there. Mother still misses Kolkata. So why not?"

"Life's not a game where you can go back and forth whenever you want."

"Well, nothing is decided yet. I'm just toying with the idea. And you're the first person I'm telling."

"Is it the NSF thing that's making you consider such a decision?"

"Maybe."

"You can't give in like this," Shelley said. "It's a retreat."

"Retreat?" Manick cried. "You haven't been where I've been. You haven't swallowed the shards of humiliation the way I have. You want to fight? Who will you fight against? The governor? The dictator president? This country, mark my words, has no future. And the six-point movement we are working on will change nothing in the end."

"I know it sounds impossible. But we have to stand against the injustice. What do you suggest otherwise? Give it all up and suck our thumbs?"

"I suggest nothing. As I see it, no fresh hope's awaiting us, either. The path's getting deeper and darker. You can call me an escapist or an opportunist. Whatever. I don't want to squander my life in a country where West Wing people think of us as inferior. Okay, you say we have to earn our rights. It's been over twenty years since Partition. What earnings do we have? Nearly nothing. And this country has become nothing but a problem child."

"That's why you're going to America?"

Manick chuckled. "Let me grab the best life has to offer me."

Shelley snorted, with a twisted smile. Manick was being selfish, he thought. When public unrest was growing, he was retiring, wishing to secure his future in America because he figured that East Pakistan would gain nothing in the end. If Shelley had done the same thing, some of his buddies would have called him names behind his back: Shala Hindu! Doesn't care about Pakistan!

Then it struck Shelley that Manick had every reason to seize the opportunities that life was offering him. Who would he burn the offerings of his life for? He hadn't lost anyone or anything. Yes, he'd endured humiliation at the hands of NSF boys. As a matter of fact, there was nothing he could do to wreak vengeance on them. If he was frustrated about that and had made his choice not to waste his time on protests, why reproach him? A good deal of students kept off rallies and marches and strikes. No one reproved them.

Manick had chosen his path. But for Shelley, the fight was not solely his fight. The back of his neck grew hot as he flashed back to the morning when Roxana had been carried off to Gopala while he was behind bars. Despite his marital conversion, he hadn't been able to keep Roxana. The lonely face of his baba came to his mind. It was this country that had torn apart his family. Shelley's fight was the fight that his baba had left behind for him. Shelley's fight was the fight that Roxana had sacrificed her life for. And he must win it.

"What are you thinking?" Manick was gazing at him steadily.

Shelley eased his clenched palm and slowly shook his head.

Silence again. Shelley shifted uncomfortably. Then asked, "How's Maya doing?"

Manick waggled his head. "Last week she had me take her to New Market. She bought a bunch of Islamic titles. Books on hadith, the Quran, the Prophet, and so forth. She's turned too religious. She prays five times a day. And when she isn't praying, she is seen with those books reading, or with tasbih prayer beads in hand."

Shelley listened and waited to hear more.

"I now try not to run into her. She has asked me to start praying. She lectured me twice about the temporariness of this life and the eternal life awaiting us. Can you imagine?"

Shelley could not. He stared in disbelief.

"She might give you some advice, too. Anyway, let me call her." Manick left the room.

He returned after a few minutes, with a roll of posters in hand. He sat down with a sigh. "She won't come now."

Now? Did she say that? Shelley did not ask.

"Here, the posters." Manick handed him the roll. "She did a nice job. Give these to Asad."

Shelley took the thick, heavy roll and asked, "How's her health? I mean mentally."

Manick shrugged. "I don't know. She seems all right apart from the divine madness. Maybe this sudden path of devoutness is doing some good to her. In some way. You know what I mean."

Shelley did understand what he meant.

"And not to mention," Manick went on, "she stopped listening to music. I guess when you see her next, she will be fully covered. My sister, can you imagine?" He groaned. "It's sheer extremism. This religious fervor is nothing but a bad fever."

Shelley remained silent. He wondered if he would ever see Maya again. The old, ordinary Maya, hair uncovered, striding boldly around. The gutsy girl who not long ago had wished to join him to attend protests and shout slogans at the top of her lungs.

CHAPTER NINE

1

It was around ten when Shelley got home from Iqbal Hall. There was a letter waiting for him inside the gate. A letter from his father. The envelope was heavy. And the letter was long. The longest ever.

He began reading. It was about Roxana's father. The man had gone crazy. Behaving oddly. Such a beefy tiger man now cowered like a cat. He had been the talk of the town for more than two months. Baba described everything in detail.

Finishing the letter, Shelley imagined it, tried to turn the words into a moving picture. Images started to roll in his head, like a real movie.

After morning prayer, Roxana's father was out for a walk. The eastern sky yawned with amber light when he strolled past the tal palm tree. He spotted a woman by the banana grove. She was standing with her back to him.

"Who are you?" he demanded, reaching the banana grove. "Who are you? Turn around."

The figure turned around. Roxana! It was Roxana!

A second or two elapsed. Toward the house he galloped like a frightened horse.

That night he saw her again in the bedroom. She stood in the corner with her back to him. This time she turned on her own, held him with her livid eyes.

"Go away, you bitch! You are dead!" he screamed to shoo away his daughter. He could not bear her cold, calm catlike stare. What, what did she want from him? She'd dragged his good name through the mud. Wasn't that enough? What else did his unruly daughter want now?

The imam arrived. He listened to everything. Then circled around the house, muttering to himself.

"I've protected the house. No evil spirit can enter now," the imam confirmed. He advised Roxana's father not to be left alone unaccompanied.

It worked. For a few days. But then one noon he passed out in the toilet and messed himself. Why? Roxana had loomed up behind him, almost touching him. From then on he went to the toilet keeping the door unlocked, and had his wife wait for him outside.

His wife wept. Her daughter's soul must be in pain. He had made the poor girl marry that man whose one foot was in the grave. He had made her die. The tiger man told her to stop crying. Otherwise he would send her to hell.

That night the tiger man took to his bed. His temperature rose, his hunger vanished. He started seeing Roxana everywhere. This time sitting on the bed, the next time hiding under the bed, another time suspended in the air.

The imam advised him to ask for Roxana's forgiveness and to follow various religious activities to calm down her departed soul.

On Friday, at the family's graveyard, the tiger man stood before Roxana's mound. For the first time he wept for his daughter. He confessed that he was wrong and had done an injustice to her. He asked her to forgive him. At the bazaar mosque, a special dua prayer was performed for her. Women in the house read the whole Quran. And then fed the poor.

Shelley sat to reply his father's letter. He wanted to say he'd never been so happy to hear about someone's misery. But he said not a word about Roxana's father. He wrote about the ongoing protests, growing public anger, and a probable civil disorder. He mentioned King Siraj. How the stifling political climate had turned a street boy like Siraj into an unwavering round-the-clock activist.

2

King Siraj befriended a stray dog. It had been dogging him for a few days, and he named it Tommy.

The late afternoon sun, outside Madhur Canteen, hung behind the mango tree. And under the tree Shelley stood smoking, watching King Siraj and his dog frolicking in the dozing light.

"Hey, who owns this Bengal hound?" A hand slapped Shelley on his shoulder.

Shelley wheeled around. It was Fourqan.

"Bengal hound?" Shelley cocked his eyebrow.

"A Sarail hound, more precisely. Originally it hailed from Sarail, Brahmanbaria. It's a good racing dog. I have two of this kind at home."

"Oh, really?" Shelley said.

"Basically they're a fusion of English greyhounds and Arabian hounds with our wild dogs."

Shelley took a good look at the dog. The black-and-white dog was long bodied, bright eyed, long legged, and had a thin, long tail with a white streak at the tip.

"You stupid dog," cried King Siraj, "behave yourself!" He was sharing bread with his pet. "You know who I am? I am King Sirajuddaula. King of Bengal. King of the world."

Tommy did not seem to be interested in his words but in bread.

"You hear? You have to bow to me every time I call you. You hear?" King Siraj twisted Tommy's ear.

"King Siraj," Fourqan called out.

The boy looked up, grinned. His white teeth glistened between his lips.

"Sell me the dog. He's disobeying the King." Fourqan made the boy an offer.

"Nah, I won't sell Tommy. He's my friend." The boy stroked the Sarail hound's long head and ears. The hound replied by wiggling its tail.

Shelley smiled. He had never seen the boy this happy.

—

That night Shelley had a dream about King Siraj. The little boy came up to him crying, holding his hand over a bleeding eye. He said that during the demonstration he'd gotten hit in the eye with a broken brick.

When Shelley woke up, he went over his dream. He wondered why the boy had taken to him. Did the boy have a strange sensitivity? Or perhaps the boy detected something in his eyes—tenderness and benevolence. Just as Tommy had in King Siraj's eyes.

The following day Shelley asked the boy where he slept at night. King Siraj replied with a typical Bengali phrase: "Wherever I lay my head at night is home."

"Where exactly is that?"

"Railway station. Buriganga port. Mosques."

"I see. Listen, you can sleep at my place from tomorrow onward," Shelley said.

"I'm fine, Shelley sir. Please don't take the trouble."

"It's no trouble. You come sleep at night and leave early in the morning."

"Okay. Are you coming to the afternoon's rally, sir?"

"Of course." He told the boy not to be too naughty, too bold in the protests. Things were different now. The police opened fire. People got killed. Army and police—all their brains could do was pull a trigger. They shot before they thought. So don't gamble your life away, he advised the boy.

—

Shelley returned to Madhur Canteen after the protest rally with the others. In the evening King Siraj showed up. His eyes were tearful. He pointed to Tommy by the door. Bewildered, Shelley gazed at the dog. The corner of its left eye was swollen, and blood had dried in a thin line. His vision appeared fine, though.

Today's protest rally had ended up with a small clash with the police. Nothing new. Tommy had shadowed King Siraj the whole time. Somehow a brickbat had struck his eye during the action.

"Don't worry, the injury isn't serious," Fourqan said, checking the wound. "Go wash him off."

The boy went out with his dog.

"There's nothing like throwing bricks at the police," said Fourqan.

"It's kind of thrilling, yes," Shelley approved. "I wouldn't blame the boy if he considers it an exciting sport."

"It's 100 percent halal," Fourqan claimed. "These police, where do their salaries come from? From our tax money. We East Wing people pay for them. And they thank us using the baton on our backs."

"They carry out orders. Humble servants of the West Wing rulers," Asad remarked.

"This is pure prostitution."

"Indeed," Asad said. "We are breaking our heads, crying for

'autonomy, autonomy.' Whether autonomy comes or not, the police will always be police. And their prostitution will always be continued for the ruling class. For the bourgeois."

"Ah, don't bring your class conflict here." Fourqan was nettled. "Our problem isn't there. Ours is the disparity between the East and the West. It's the power conflict. And autonomy is the sole solution."

The argument went on. Partition. Gandhi, Jinnah, Subhas Bose jumped on the table.

3

The necklace looked good on Roxana. The artificial pearl gave her a goddess-like glamour. Shelley had bought it from a street shop.

"I'm sorry," he said to the statue, "from tomorrow we won't be seeing each other at night."

He whistled a tune. "Eight Days a Week." He settled down at his desk to go over the day's class lecture. He glanced back at Roxana. Lately he had been having a bizarre sensation whenever he was at home. He felt Roxana's unblinking eyes watching him all the time, following him everywhere around the room.

He looked at the yellow poster on the left wall. He'd kept one of Maya's handwritten posters. The huge letters in black ink read:

Your tongue
My tongue
Bangla, Bangla

The next evening Shelley arrived home around ten with King Siraj. He offered the boy a mat, a pillow, and a bedspread to cover up his body from mosquito bites. The boy took a look at the floor, said it was clean and perfect. He needed nothing. Shelley insisted. The boy then spread out the mat and sat on it, but did not lie down.

"Shelley sir."

"Hmm."

"What if Tommy goes blind?"

"He won't. We can take him for a checkup at the veterinary hospital. The one in Nimtoli. You've seen it?"

"Yeah."

The room darkened as Shelley blew out the hurricane lamp. He wondered about Tommy, who was outside on the veranda. He heard the hound scratch the doorstep.

The first thing Shelley heard the next morning was barking. He peered out of the window and spotted the Bengal hound trotting up and down. Tommy was growling at a monkey sitting on a neighbor's roof. This part of old Dhaka had primates. They nicked food, even pickle jars from the kitchen. He heard that they occasionally took clothes as ransom and would return them for food.

Apart from his half-shut red, swollen eye, Shelley found Tommy pretty healthy. Traveling with Tommy was no good, King Siraj told him after waking. Before he had Tommy, he rode on the backs of rickshaws or horse carriages without being noticed by drivers. Now, as the dog ran beside him, the drivers spotted him straight away. Therefore, no more free travel for King Siraj.

—

At Sharif Mia's Canteen, Shelley had tea with Manick. This was their new meeting spot as Manick had distanced himself from the Madhur Canteen crowd.

"You're not studying much, Shelley."

Shelley eyed him comically. Fresh off the library, Manick smelled of books. The sides of his nose were oily.

"It's okay. I don't fancy a first," Shelley explained.

"You're being absurd."

"It's all right."

"It's not all right. It's crap. Politics. Who are you squandering your life for? This country is diseased. The Promised Land will sink." He was at it again.

"Never lose hope, Manick. Look around. People are rising. Big Brother President must step down."

"Seriously, you believe his fall will change everything? The East Wing will be given autonomy and all?"

"It'll be a breakthrough, of course."

"A breakthrough. And that's it. No more. Period. People's dreams will go away, give up the ghost."

"Every dream looks distant when you start dreaming. But it'll seem like magic when you get there in the end," Shelley continued. "Rights have to be earned, not served before you on a plate."

Manick rubbed his oily nose. "Wish I could join you on the journey, but I don't feel like it."

"It's fine. You follow your heart. We miss you anyway."

Manick shrugged.

During their second round of tea, King Siraj rushed up. Behind him was his dog, racing up, too.

"What're you up to, boy?" Shelley hollered, craning his neck forward.

"You chill o-out here? Police just gun-nned down someone in Palashi." With sporadic stammering, King Siraj delivered his message in one breath. And spat through his teeth after the delivery.

Everyone at the canteen clustered around him. But the boy was unable to give any details. He'd heard the shot with his own ears and picked up the rest from the crowd. A group of demonstrators, he said, were crossing the street. The police didn't attempt to disperse them. Nor did they fire tear gas. They shot first.

"Okay, see you later," Shelley said to Manick, and along with others he flew to Palashi.

4

It was not long before students and the general public took to the streets. Some said a young boy had been shot in the hand and taken to the hospital. The injury was not serious. Others said the boy had been shot in the chest and had died on the way to the hospital. But whatever had happened, it had happened to kill Bengalis. Shouts filled the air, drowning out police whistles.

Palashi and its vicinity turned into a battlefield. At Palashi intersection, police had blocked the road. Shelley did what the others were doing. Threw brickbats at the police. King Siraj helped him with the ammunition supply. Somebody fetched a tire and set fire to it. Others put rubbish on it to increase the flame. Clouds of black smoke blossomed into a colossal monster in the sky. Slogans were shouted:

"Break the prison lock! Bring the leader back!"

"Down, down, down with autocracy! We want autonomy, autonomy!"

One voice in the mob said that they should go siege the governor's house. A small crowd cried back instantly, assenting to this proposition. Hollering slogans, they moved forward a little. Some had bamboo sticks in their raised hands. Those bamboo-filled hands showed such an appetite for annihilation that surely the governor's residence was going to fall apart today. A few strikes—as if that were all the palace needed to cry in pain, to go to pieces.

"Tear gas, tear gas!" voices shouted.

"Shelley! Shelley! Come this way." Asad pulled Shelley toward Nilkhet Road.

One tear gas shell landed near King Siraj. The little warrior picked up the burning shell and lobbed it back at the police. He did it with such promptness that Shelley could not forbid him. Two more shells fell from the sky. The police were starting to move in. Their batons blazed in the air. Amid baton charges at the front and tear gas in the middle, the mob retreated, resigned, dashed away in every direction.

At a safe distance Shelley and Asad stopped to catch their breath. They panted, took breaths with open mouths. King Siraj looked fine, kept spitting through his teeth. Across the street Shelley made out a senior student from his department who was hunkering down and gasping for air. He had asthma. Shelley scurried up to him. "You okay?" He patted him on the back.

"Absolutely," the senior said, still wheezing with labored breath.

"You sure?"

"Very much. Look at your foot."

Shelley looked down and found that his right foot was missing its sandal. He didn't know how that had happened.

"Guess what's the benefit of getting regularly chased by the police?" the senior asked.

"What is it?"

"You're ready for the Olympic marathon."

Shelley laughed.

"King Sirajuddaula!" the senior called to the boy.

King Siraj stepped forward.

"Again, you have been defeated at the Battle of Plassey."

"No, sir," said the boy. "Shall I go release m-my fart-bomb?"

"Make it an atomic fart-bomb," the senior said. "But dialogue first."

Before him King Siraj got down on one knee and commenced to deliver the likable and lovable lines from the film *Nawab Sirajuddaula.* "O the great ruler of Bangla, Bihar, and Orissa, I've not forgotten your last advice, sir. You said do not tolerate the East India Company. You said they'll try everything to take over the country. I will not tolerate them at any cost, sir." His presentation was free of stuttering.

Whoops and cheers came from a few more people around them, who also started clapping. Another silent observer, Tommy, barked softly in a singsong. He had become slow and quiet, and his left eye had swollen half shut. Thick pus drained from the wound.

"He's lost his appetite," King Siraj reported later.

The Bengal hound looked droopy and barked dully. Shelley worried this time. "Tomorrow we'll try to take him to a vet."

But tomorrow came and went. Then another day.

At the time, Dhaka was an anarchic city. A city of awakened souls versus the autocratic government. When human lives were becoming numbers, just the dust of memories, who cared about a mere wounded dog? Shelley didn't. Nor did King Siraj have time to chew on it.

5

Shelley was having breakfast with buttered toast at Sharif Mia's Canteen. Fourqan walked in and waited for him to finish.

"What is it?" Shelley asked.

"Let's take a walk." Across the canteen they walked on the grass.

"What's up?"

Fourqan glanced around and said, "The police may bust us."

"Us? Who is us? You and me?"

"No. Us. Our group."

"Why the hell would the police do that? We've never damaged any state properties. Never set fire to a double-decker bus."

"You silly ass," Fourqan said. "The mad dog president's got rabies. His tongue's sticking out as he tries to tackle the turmoil. Even the police are running away from his angry bite."

"And that's why you think the police will crash into us?"

Fourqan laughed. "The reality is the police are under huge pressure. Panicky. Now they shit their pants when protesters go berserk."

"Ordinary people make them poop in their pants, too."

"To avoid that mess, they consider random arrests as the only solution. So they can stop any students from getting involved in the movement."

"On the contrary," said Shelley, "it rather triggers the movement. And people go ballistic."

"Exactly. The government's gone too frantic to grasp this."

"But why do you think the police will arrest us particularly?"

"They might not. But there's a possibility. They won't do it from the campus anyway. Because you know how students are reacting at present."

"How do you know this?"

"Listen, this is a deadly secret." Fourqan scratched his temple. "I have a Bihari buddy working as a police source."

"A Bihari?" he scowled. He had conflicting emotions about the Biharis. He had heard, from his father, about the horror of the Adamjee Jute Mills riots in 1954. Two of his distant relatives who had worked for the mill were killed by Biharis then.

"He's not like his race anyway," Fourqan said quickly. "I've known him a long time. He occasionally passes me information."

Shelley took a silent moment. Anarchy, he thought. Protesters were being arrested on false accusations every day. The prisons were pregnant with students. "Okay," he said. "What do you suggest then?"

"I suggest we stay away from home for some time. Maybe nothing will happen. Just take it as a precaution."

They were walking toward Madhur Canteen. Shelley asked, "Think the government will set the leader free?"

"There'll be Roman fires in every stretch of the East Wing if they don't. Sheikh Mujib's release and our rights have been synonymous."

—

King Siraj showed Shelley a way out. After supper the boy suggested a mosque for them to sleep in. Shelley accepted the offer, for he did not wish to be a nuisance to any of his friends. It would only be a matter of six or seven hours, he thought. He had had the encounter of becoming a Muslim, but that had not involved the saying of prayers. He held back. "What if they find out?" he asked the boy.

"Hindus and Muslims aren't inscribed on the forehead," said King Siraj. "How would they know?"

Shelley reflected for a moment. The mosque would be better off than an open railway platform. A whole night of unbroken sleep, and all they had to do was get up before the dawn prayer. It sounded reasonable.

"Just be careful about facing the feet toward the west," King Siraj said, "where Allah sleeps. If the genies find you like that, they will break your legs."

Hindu texts suggested otherwise, Shelley thought. If a man slept with his head westward or northward, he became diseased. A phrase in one language got mistranslated into another language. The Bengali proverb crossed his mind.

The boy took him to Binat Bibi Mosque, close to the neighborhood. There was a nice star-shaped water reservoir inside. Often, he had glimpsed it while walking past the place.

"This is for ablution," the boy told him.

"I know." He saw some fish swimming in it.

The mosaic floor of the vestibule-cum-veranda was cold to sleep on.

"In a pullover, you won't feel cold at all," King Siraj assured.

Shelley spotted a bearded man, only in a shirt, already there, dead to the world. The night was quiet, touched by the interruption of infrequent passing vehicles on the adjacent street. Hands behind his head, Shelley drifted off to sleep.

6

King Siraj had made a vow. He would, no matter what, injure a policeman in the eye. His pockets and a small carrier bag in his hand were stuffed with high-quality brickbats.

"They wear helmets, shields," Shelley reminded him.

"Whatever. I'll make it," King Siraj said. His tone was venomous. "I've pra-a-acticed a lot."

"Careful. Things will get really bad today. Tomorrow's the hartal."

It was Friday, the protestors' presence palpable on the thoroughfares. Within spitting distance of the medical college, the police had blocked the strike marchers. So the battle of brickbats began. The crowds were bowling. The police were batting, defensive. It was a match, a tug of war. When the police stepped forward, the protesters stepped backward. And vice versa. In between, the police swooped on one of the protesters, a law student. They dragged him away and threw him in the back of a pickup van like a sack. The hail of brickbats from

King Siraj failed to stop them and shatter their helmets. He shrieked slogans. The tendons in his throat showed every time his balled fist struck the air.

Shelley noticed some policemen turning, looking all around them. He caught sight of the other side of the road. Another student demo was closing in. This meant the police would be in the middle, dealing with marchers on both sides, trapped. It was a rare event that he had never encountered. He spotted King Siraj advancing toward the police who were standing in a line. "Hey!" he called to the boy. "Don't go so close."

King Siraj ceased ten yards away from the police. The next second Shelley found the boy standing in the middle of the road, urinating facing the police. "To hell with you," he shouted at them.

The marchers behind King Siraj burst with laughter. But that ended abruptly as the police set to move. The police pickup vans groaned. Their whistles blew, and their batons began to swing.

"Off! This way. That way." Cries broke out in the crowd. Two or three protesters went red, wet with blood. King Siraj was nowhere. Then a couple of gunshots. A moment of silence. Then shouting, squawking.

When the police moved on again, King Siraj was seen lying on the ground, bleeding. The glaring sun shone on the boy's parted lips, on his blood-soaked shirt. The little boy, like a little dead bird, was lying flat and faceup. Before Shelley realized, a crowd gathered around the boy. Shelley's hands and the hands of others carried King Siraj. He was still as a log when the stretcher ferried him into the emergency room. Lingering at the emergency door, Shelley heard the hovering voices around him.

"Think the boy will survive?"

"He stopped breathing."

"Maybe the doctors can do something."

Barely twenty minutes had passed when the emergency room door opened and a young doctor's face appeared. The noise in the corridor stopped all at once.

"Sorry," he said. "There was nothing we could do."

"What do you mean there was nothing you could do?" Shelley demanded.

"He was dead on the spot."

Shelley looked to the crowd for help. They were mute, motionless. From the corridor vent there came the chattering sound of sparrows. He felt a hand on his back.

"Does the boy have anyone close we can inform?" Asad asked.

Shelley shook his head.

"Then we should arrange for a funeral prayer," someone suggested.

But they soon discovered that walking out of the hospital with the dead body was impossible. Plenty of police had cordoned off the building. No marching or carrying the dead, they'd declared.

It turned out the dead body needed to have a postmortem performed. A police order the hospital was bound to follow. What use was a dissection? Shelley blew up. The police had killed King Siraj. It was as clear as day. So why? Would the Yama or Angel of Death ask for an autopsy report to enter the grave?

"The police are panicking now," one student leader said. "They're simply procrastinating."

Asad suggested they join the protests outside. The autopsy would take time.

"I'll stay a while," Shelley said.

—

Stories went around of King Siraj's glorious life and times. The boy had been ingenious. A born activist. Loved protests more than food. Another brave Khudiram. The governor ought to learn patriotism from this little boy.

Later, a young doctor informed Shelley that after the postmortem the dead body could be claimed only by the boy's parents. If they failed to show up, the police would bury the corpse.

7

Azimpur Graveyard. With the help of a gravedigger, Shelley located King Siraj's whereabouts. And there he was surprised to find Tommy napping by the grave. The hound jumped up and approached him, wagging his tail. Shelley got a welcoming wet nose nudging his hand. He squatted and petted the hound for a while.

Tommy's left eye had returned to its normal shape, but it looked cloudy. A small ashy pearl had developed inside his iris. Shelley waved his hand before that eye. No response. Presumably it had lost vision. Shelley sighed. "I'm sorry, my friend."

King Siraj's new residence was at the poorest ghetto where unclaimed bodies populated. Nonetheless there were trees, soft shadows, tall grasses, and a bed of dry leaves all around. Shelley noted that an earthworm was crawling across the boy's burial mound.

"You see, King Siraj," Shelley said, squatting by the grave mound, "there's this green garden between you and me. Between being and nothingness is just the distance of a garden. Nothing else."

He spotted a skull peeping out in the adjoining burial row. The skull, small, caked in dust and dirt, had full teeth. Shelley drew near, searched for the body that went with it. Nothing. There must be jackals here, he thought. Or body snatchers who emerged after nightfall.

Maybe by selling the earthly remains they made the dead feel worthwhile, valuable.

A memory struck him. In his village school, there was a human skeleton in the lab. He had always felt immensely sorry for that dead man's remains. When alive had he ever imagined, Shelley used to wonder, that his remains would be hung up and exposed to educate his own species? What a miserable eternal afterlife! It was because of that hanging skeleton that Shelley didn't take science in school. Science meant working with dead remains—this assumption killed him. Plus, the class captain, Kaiser, told him that it was the skeleton of the date-juice collector of the village, who had died falling from a tree. There was a remarkable fracture in the skull, so the possibility couldn't be ruled out.

Tommy trailed after Shelley, wagging his tail to the edge of the graveyard.

"Come, I'll buy you some food," Shelley offered. But the hound wouldn't leave the premises.

Traffic was slow on the road; a protest march was up ahead. Shelley noticed a bunch of street kids shouting different slogans. These days it was a trendy sport for them. The slogans were all funny, such as: "Slap the Khans' cheeks with shoes, with shoes!" This was literally impossible, because all these stray children were barefooted.

Shelley went to New Market and wandered about. For the first time since Roxana's death, it occurred to him that he had nowhere to go to spend the afternoon. No one expected his visits anymore. As if he had become a nonperson.

Shelley ceased before a store, knives at the glass window caught his eye. "GOOD FOREIGN KNIVES SOLD HERE" read the sign on the door. He thought of King Siraj. The boy had once asked him to buy him a knife to kill KK.

Shelley glided into the store asked if they had pocketknives. The salesman demonstrated one type to him. "It's called a Swiss army knife. Very handy," the man said. It had other tools, too. Scissors, a screwdriver, a bottle opener. But the main tool, the knife, was a small blade. Less than two inches.

"Do you have any others?" Shelley asked.

The salesman then showed him jackknives. He checked the one with a blade hidden inside a wooden handle. A five-inch straight-back blade seemed satisfactory. He bought it.

PART
THREE

CHAPTER TEN

1

There wasn't much to do in the *Cinemagazine* office today. The last issue had come out two days ago. Shelley half finished a follow-up story, read the day's newspaper, smoked two cigarettes, and then set off.

In the late softening daylight outside, he walked about the lonely Johnson Road. Some days, if he finished work early, he hit the neighboring public library, either Northbrook Hall or Brahmo Samaj. These places were fabulous for lingering over old books and periodicals. Sometimes he would just go and leaf through the grizzled pages and inhale the smell of history, rather than longing to read them.

He felt no urge to make his way there today. A protest march was passing him. He trailed behind it but didn't chorus in unison. Protestors chanted the familiar slogans, throwing their hands up in the air. Their heated words failed to invigorate Shelley. He thought about Manick. Perhaps his prophecy would come true. All these demonstrations and the blood of lives would bring no change in the end. The destiny of the people of East Pakistan would remain same.

He cut loose from the march in Ray Shaheb Bazaar, where protestors paused to set ablaze the dictator. Ayub Khan's photos and a copy of his book *Friends Not Masters* were burned. A batch of teenagers came out cheering as they had just taken down a framed photo of Ayub Khan from a restaurant. They spat in the face of the dictator with wild joy. They dropped the photo frame, trampled it, and then threw it into the fire.

The thrill and delight of the protestors, seeing Ayub Khan in flames, turned the Ray Shaheb Bazaar roundabout into an effervescent spot. The acrid smell stirred Shelley's memories of King Siraj. Had King Siraj been here at this moment, Shelley reflected, maybe the boy could have perked up the crowd doing something classic; the boy wouldn't have forgotten to piss in the face of the dictator. Shelley smiled and turned right on English Road.

—

Shelley waited a few seconds before the gate. He lifted his hand to knock on the door of Dream Garden. Something stopped him. A zillion seconds zipped by, and he didn't knock. You're not welcome here anymore, a voice inside him reverberated. A heavy sigh emanated from his heart. He turned around to hit the road.

A feeling of orphancy pierced him. There was no one waiting for him. No one. There was nowhere he could go. Nowhere. In the chilly air he trudged down the road to his home.

2

Shelley took ample time to clothe Roxana with her best clothes. The sari this time, with perfect pleats, was wrapped around her waist. He carefully applied an ox-red lipstick over her mouth. He placed the chair before the statue and seated himself. Did the red lipstick match with her skin color? He lit a cigarette and thought.

He stubbed out the cigarette and grabbed a rag to wipe off the lipstick. But he leaned over and placed his mouth on hers, softly rubbing. He remembered the first night with Roxana—their bridal night. When he had kissed her reddened lips, the lipstick smeared on his lips, too. He let out a sigh and gazed at Roxana.

"Roxana!" he said. "Do you think I'm unlucky? Whoever gets close to me dies. Am I really unlucky?" Roxana's eyes were locked on his. "Please answer me. I can't take it anymore." His eyes welled with tears. He buried his face in his hands.

Shelley heard a soft, imperceptible voice. He jerked in his chair and nearly fell from it. His heart stopped.

"Roxana!" he found his voice saying. "Is it you? Really you?"

Roxana gave an enigmatic smile. He eyed her lithe body in the ivory sari. She was standing two feet away from him, her body weight on her left foot. He rose from his chair. "Can I touch you?"

Roxana shook her head.

"Why, honey?"

"You know why. Our paths have parted."

Shelley sighed deeply.

"You were being naughty the other night," she said in a silky tone.

"What, honey?"

"You were doing something with me. Forgot? You were—"

"Oh, oh. I'm . . . I'm sorry."

"Don't be. It's fine." Roxana smiled seductively.

Shelley saw her gleaming dimples. She hadn't changed at all.

"I want you to be happy. Don't ever think that you are unlucky."

"I feel so miserable, so alone, Roxana."

"You'll be okay. Don't fret." A pause. "It's late, get some sleep."

"I can't sleep."

"Try."

"Will you sleep with me?"

"It won't do any good, honey." Roxana took a step back. "Try to get some sleep. Good night, my love."

Before Shelley could utter "no," he found Roxana in her unmoving figure, standing in her usual posture. He stepped up and touched her face. "Roxana! Roxana!"

The statue in the ivory sari did not stir. Roxana's face was stony and still. Shelley plopped down on the bed. Half lying there, he stared at Roxana's lifeless figure. He lay awake until dawn, smoking and looking at her.

—

The following afternoon, Shelley didn't find Tommy in Azimpur Graveyard. He had brought some cutlets for him. He waited twenty minutes, sitting by King Siraj's grave, to no avail.

Shelley strolled about the graveyard. He came across some graves of notable names. Some had brick walls around them. Some had only the headstone. A sobbing sound caught his ear. He noticed a few people some twenty yards away under a jackfruit tree. A dead body had just been buried, he figured. Father? Mother? Brother? Or someone's husband? Or wife? Shelley longed to know, but he didn't budge.

The sun was falling, a honey-yellow ball hanging in the sky. Now a golden disc above the horizon. He stepped nearer a mango tree that seemed to be home to a sparrow colony. The homecoming cries of the creatures were loud and lively. When there was the call for the Maghrib prayers, he returned to King Siraj's site. Tommy wasn't back yet. Dusk was fast descending on the earth. He had never understood why the setting sun moved so fast in the last few minutes.

He left the paper sack of cutlets by the grave.

3

The atmosphere of Madhur Canteen was fevered and fiery, buzzing with students. It indicated that the political temperature of the country was scalding hot. Shelley found his mates at a table next to the food counter. He shared a seat with Fourqan.

"You're a weird guy," Fourqan said.

"Why?"

"In this high time of protests, you've vanished. I don't understand you. Sometimes you're too active, sometimes not."

Shelley shrugged.

Fourqan poured some tea into his saucer and slurped it. "Well, I'm sorry for your little friend. We all miss King Siraj. But it's not the time for mourning. You and Manick, I don't understand .... People are about to topple the dictator, and you two—"

"Ah, let them be." Asad raised his hand at Fourqan. "Shelley, you want tea?"

Shelley gave a nod.

"Are you all right? Your eyes look red."

"Oh, it's just . . . I didn't have a good sleep last night," Shelley said.

—

From Madhur Canteen Shelley made his way to Palashi Bazaar for dinner. There was a particular café where the okra bhaji dish was his favorite—it gave him the taste of his mother's okra dish.

He sauntered down dimly lit Fuller Road. Flanked by university staff quarters and the British Council library, Fuller Road had a veritable aura of the "Oxford of the East" elegance. This wondrous road in the heart of the university campus was exceptionally quiet, and it got really cold in the winter evening. Shelley wrapped his shawl around his head to keep his ears warm. There was a bracing aromatic fragrance in the air; it must be kamini flowers.

Next to the British Council, Shelley took the shortcut across SM Hall to get to Palashi. The path through the trees was dark. If it had been monsoon season, he wouldn't have dared take it for fear of snakes. Just then a cussing voice from the road shattered the silence of the whole neighborhood: *Abbey motherchod, jorey chaala.* The yelling was directed at a rickshawwallah for failing to drive fast.

Shelley's feet slowed. That cussing voice sounded familiar. As he closed in toward the dorm's facade, he caught a rickshaw with two passengers coming through the grandiose main gate of SM Hall. Shortly the rickshaw glided past him on the driveway, and the evening cold whipped his face. He paused.

The three-wheeler pulled in right by the softly lit arched entrance of the dorm. Two figures jumped out of the passenger seat and strutted down the corridor.

"Where's my fare?" the rickshawwallah hollered.

One figure halted, whirled around, and returned straight back up to the asker. Without warning, the flat of his hand landed on the rickshaw man's sunken cheek.

"You motherchod. Don't you know who I am?"

The second figure joined him, whacked the man's other cheek. "We never pay fares. Remember us!"

Though taken aback by the peculiar form of payment, the poor man's dignity rose up, lifted its head in no time. "Why hit me? Better to just say you can't pay!"

It ticked them off. They pummeled his face and head. The rickshawwallah inched away, covering his face with his arms.

Shelley recognized the NSF boys—KK and his companion.

The noise of the beating of the rickshaw man—the pounding cacophony—was sickening on the quiet evening. The overpowering sound of slapping and smacking seared Shelley. All at once, the ordeal of the rickshaw man reminded him of the moment at the police station. He saw Roxana's face before his eyes. He felt her touch, her firm grip on his arm. But he was being dragged away by a policeman . . .

Shelley was breathing noisily. His nostrils flared. He briskly broke out of his spell. His hand fiddled around in his pocket. He drew out the knife and opened the blade. The touch of the knife, the feel of the sharp silver blade heated him and shook him like an explosion.

"Stop it," shouted Shelley, his hand with the knife behind his shawl.

The beating stopped at once. All eyes were set on Shelley.

"Who the fuck are you?" KK said, stepping forward. He stood before Shelley. "Ooh! You Hindu motherchod." He seized Shelley by the collar and slapped him across the face. "Shala malaun."

With astonishing rapidity, Shelley thrust the knife into KK's neck. KK let out a sharp cry, his grip loosening on Shelley's collar. Pulling out his knife, Shelley struck again almost in the same spot, harder than the first time. Blood spurted.

"You motherchod!" Shelley shouted back with the third strike. KK collapsed on his tush, moaning miserably.

KK's companion, shocked and stunned, didn't dare move for a second. Shelley held his gaze. The man bolted down the driveway like a madman.

"I'll kill you, motherchod," KK grunted in his anguished voice, one hand over his neck wound and the other on the ground.

Shelley gritted his teeth, his grip on the hilt fiercer. He thrust the knife upward into KK's throat. The knife stuck there, piercing into the roof of KK's mouth. The blood gushed out from his throat as if from a shuddering sacrificial animal. Shelley eyed the hemorrhaging beast.

"Now talk, you motherchod!" He kicked him. KK landed flat on his back. His eyes bulged out of his sockets.

The rickshawwallah, bruised and with blood trickling from his nose, was watching Shelley strangely. He glanced away as Shelley looked at him. The man mopped his mouth with his hand, limped to his rickshaw, and scurried away.

Shelley gazed at the broken beast at his feet. KK was groaning, blood bubbling inside his mouth. His jaw agape with a big unuttered scream. Shelley stood, unmoved. For a fraction of a second, he felt ecstatic. He opened his mouth and sucked in air. He was hot, sweating as if it were April, even though the colossal forecourt pulsed with the evening cold, blowing waves of winter.

Shelley found his hand blood sodden. He trembled with repulsion. He couldn't look at his own hand. He leaned down and frantically wiped his hand on KK's sweater. He began shaking. He thought of breaking into a run and started, but a sudden dizziness seized him. His vision blurred. He lingered and looked around. Then, amid the growing whispers and murmurs of a sprinkling of students, he started toward the main gate. At a leisurely pace. No one stopped him. The onlookers in the corridor seemed to be delighted to see KK annihilated.

CHAPTER ELEVEN

1

Out into the night Shelley sped off. Maybe ten or twenty or thirty minutes later, he stopped and sat himself down at the side of the pavement. Head lodged between his knees, he huffed and puffed. He viewed his own shadow in the moonlight: a little lamb. He spat at it.

The desolate street from time to time was interrupted by the sound of vehicles. He was no longer panting. His heartbeat slowed. Yet there was a nonstop shaking in his legs. His hands failed to stop them. Cigarette, he needed a cigarette. Up he stood, tried to ignore the tremors. At that point the headlights of a passing car pierced him. Only then did he notice the shawl on his shoulders had a bloodstain. Dry blood, too, on the fingers of his right hand. Madly, he mopped his hand with the shawl and tossed it away in a corner. Where was this street? he asked himself. Bakshi Bazaar? Up ahead he saw a kiosk open.

At the kiosk, while lighting a cigarette from a burning jute rope, his hand shook. It's okay, it's okay, he thought. It's cold. People will think I'm cold.

"You're lighting the wrong end," he heard the kiosk man say.

"Oh." He repositioned the cigarette.

He strode down the street, legs still quivering. The acrid odor from the filter of the cigarette was oozing in his mouth. Abruptly, he stopped dead. The tremor in his legs ceased. It occurred to him that he was heading down the jail road. A five-minute walk would take him straight to the Central Jail. "What an idiot!" he said to himself.

He hopped into an oncoming rickshaw heading in the other direction.

"Go," he spat.

"Where to?" the driver asked.

"Just go."

The rickshaw tore along the night streets of Dhaka. The cold December breeze began to bite. His clothes sweat-sodden. He looked up. Up above the world, the canvas of the sky was so serene and restful. When the rickshaw rolled onto Jinnah Avenue, he spoke. "Go to Narinda Road."

—

For supper Shelley entered Bismillah Restaurant. "Pyaar kiya toh dorna kya," a song from the film *Mughal-e-Azam*, was blaring from the restaurant's cassette player. *Why should I be afraid to be in love? Why should I be afraid to be in love?* The chorus in the voice of Lata Mangeshkar reverberated along the adjacent street of the eatery. As if her voice were to do some miracle like the Emperor Akbar's legendary musician, Tansen. Shelley willed her singing to bring a rain at this time à la Tansen.

As the manager of the diner drew close to him, Shelley said out loud, "Pease stop playing this song. So earsplitting. Gives me a throbbing pain."

The manager looked him over. "Sir, are you okay?"

"Yes, why?"

"Are you not cold?"

"I'm hot, rather." His sweat-heavy shirt looked a little scruffy. He knew. But no red marks anywhere. "It's whisky. Whisky always makes me nuts." He patted the manager's upper arm, and without checking for his reaction headed for the handwashing area.

2

Before unlocking the padlock, Shelley thought twice. The police were going to be at his home sooner or later. "When they come, they come," he murmured. All he wanted now was a nice sleep. He opened the front gate, walked into the yard, and unlocked his room door. Roxana's standing figure greeted him with her muted silence. He undressed in the dark and disappeared into the bathroom to have a cold shower.

He opened a fresh Capstan pack. Cigarette in mouth, legs crossed, he installed himself on the bed. Some of his friends presumably had learned about the murder by now. And the police must be hunting for him—everywhere except at his own home. The idea of finding him in his own bed, after killing KK, would be beyond their belief. He flicked the cigarette ash on the floor. He gazed at Roxana. She seemed to be sullen. The gleam in her face was gone.

"I'm sorry, Roxana," he said. "Killing KK was not on my mind. But in that particular moment, I couldn't bear it."

Roxana's unblinking eyes outstared him.

"Maybe I shouldn't have carried the knife." He sighed. "Oh, please. Don't give me that doleful look. Think about the upshot. KK is gone. It's a watershed moment for all the student organizations. This will boldly bolster the protest movement."

He stood and picked up a tote bag from the clothes stand. In the bag lived Roxana. The things that were outliving her. Two saris, some undergarments, a petticoat, and a set of salwar kameez. Into her bras he plunged his nose, dove deep into the cups. They smelled of old clothes now, bereft of air and sun.

Shelley planted his head on the pillow. He turned and pulled out a letter from under the pillow. Roxana's last words to him. He held it out, peered at the lines in black ink. Every word of the letter was in his memory. There was nothing on this earth he had read so many times.

He woke to the sound of the door rattling. The police? Cocking his ear, he stayed still for half a minute. No rattling. He melted back into sleep. Again, he jerk-awoke hearing the sound. This happened a few more times. Then for some time everything was quiet. He heard his own gentle snoring. Then he made out a known figure. A moon-faced woman, smiling. He sat up, startled.

"Roxana!"

"Why worry, Shelley?" Roxana spoke softly in an undertone. Her countenance luminous. "You've done nothing wrong."

"You think so?"

"With all my heart."

"Thank you."

"You'll find a beautiful place," said her comforting voice.

"Where would that be?"

"Far away from this city." Roxana smiled with the corner of her mouth. "Just one request."

"What, honey?"

"Please don't leave me alone here."

"I won't, I won't."

There was a pause.

"Will you . . ." Shelley broke off. Roxana seemed to fade away into a foggy landscape. "Wait, wait . . ."

Roxana didn't wait. All Shelley could make out was Roxana's unmoved statue, a little smile on the corner of her lips.

—

Shelley heard some sounds. He opened his eyes to the sound of the waking birds. He looked next to his bed. Roxana was standing there. For a while he peered at her and listened to the predawn chorus. In prison he might never hear birds singing or see the sight of the virginal sun. He ached with desire to see the birth of a new day—a new day on the banks of the Buriganga River.

He quickly wrapped Roxana with outdated newspaper to carry her with him.

The bite-sized honey-yellow sun was rising over the Buriganga River, over the silhouette of trees. Shelley walked along the bund and came to a hushed place. He exposed Roxana's head from the paper wrapping. He stroked her face, her eyes, nose, lips. "I'm sorry, honey," he whispered. "It's the best I can do. I promised I wouldn't leave you there." A cry pooled at the depths of his throat. He kissed Roxana on her lips, and tossed her into the river. With the sound of a big splash, the statue drowned in the waters of Buriganga.

3

Sitting on the shore, Shelley was gazing in the horizon, lost in the white magic of the newborn sun. His meditation was broken by a woman's repeated voice.

"Hey, mister!"

He looked. Ahead stood a woman soaked to the skin. The morning river was dripping like dew from her hair, her sari.

"Hey, mister! What you looking at there?"

Her words floated like water vapor when she repeated them. Was she a nymph? he wondered. Who would dare to have a cold river bath at this time of the year? It took him a while to realize that she was a woman of human flesh. The bather wrung out her dripping hair. She stepped aside and turned around. Facing the river, she began to change her clothes.

He sat undecided, dazed. The woman was in her mid-twenties. She wrapped a dry sari around her shoulder that shrouded her upper half. Beneath it she removed her sopping blouse and put on a dry one. Then she released her sodden sari, with her long petticoat underneath it, and swiftly slipped into a dry one. Moments later she walked up to him, cool and fully dressed. In a white-and-red sari, she was dazzling. She had Anglo-Indian fair skin, an oblong face, thin lips, and a pointy nose. The morning sun reflected on her silver earrings.

"What do you watch here?" she asked. Her soggy hair was wrapped in a cotton towel. Although nosy, there was a comforting wave in her words.

Shelley did not answer.

"Want some tea?"

To her flirtatious offer, he nodded slightly.

She walked over to the nearby tea vendor, leaving her river-drenched clothes and her smell with him. He watched her. It was magnetic, the way she walked, and the way her hips understood her steps.

"Hooker! Kandupatti hooker!" He heard a squeaking voice behind him. He turned. A wiry old man stood next to him, brushing his teeth with a twig. His scarf sat around his head as a hat.

"Prostituting all night, they come here to get cleaned. And pollute the river." The man spat hard.

"Isn't the water cold?" Shelley asked.

"These tarts feel no cold. They have fire mines fitted in their privates." The man scrubbed his front teeth with the tooth stick. "Careful, these girls are evil."

As the evil girl was reappearing, the man moved toward the prostitute-polluted river to rinse his mouth out.

A cup in either hand, the woman returned. Shelley took one cup. She settled herself beside him.

"I've seen you before." She slurped her tea. "Interestingly, you look like my brother."

He glanced at her sidelong, realizing the reason for her buying him tea. Where possibly had she seen him? By the river some other time? Checking out old books and magazines in the street on the way there?

"Will you come here tomorrow as well?

He gave a slight nod.

"What's wrong with you? It hurts if you talk?"

Shelley flashed a tight smile and regarded her. She appeared no different from any other household woman. A pretty, neighborly face. And quite attractive too. Once or twice, he recalled, he'd happened to pass the brothel on English Road. Women with excessive makeup and excessively reddened lips waved to him from a distance. That was all. Now, sitting next to him, this woman did not look like them.

"No, I'm just . . . not in a talking mood," he said.

"Not in a talking mood?" She laughed. "You must be a poet!"

"What makes you think I'm a poet?"

"You have a definite look of a poet. I can tell."

He checked his ash-gray pullover, his khaki chinos. He felt his face with the flat of his hand. "I haven't shaved for a week."

"You're funny, like . . ."

"Like?"

"Never mind. No, it's not the beard that gives you the poetic effect. Look, everyone around you is doing something. Only you, this early morning, are watching the river. Doing nothing. And when I was bathing, you didn't even look at me." She slurped from her cup noisily as she spoke. Her fingernails were dirty, and her red nail polish was peeling off.

He lit a cigarette.

"May I have one?"

He handed her one and the match.

Her match-striking and cigarette-lighting seemed professional, but her puffing was amateurish.

"I saw you in the protest," she blurted.

Such an incredible memory, he thought. Then he realized she had said he resembled her brother. "You go to protests?"

"Sometimes. If I run into a march, I join. It feels good." She laughed. "Often, I stop by Victoria Park if there's something going on. I love listening to what they say."

He was amazed.

The quiet puffing continued.

"You asked why I'm here," he said. "You want the honest answer?"

She looked at him inquiringly.

"I'm on the run."

"Why?" Her eyes narrowed but didn't wait long for his reply. Slapping the air, she said, "I get it. These days they're putting everyone in jail. On the last hartal day, I was out in the street to picket. A policeman almost caught me. But I outran him. Hehe."

He joined her in laughing.

She sipped the last bit of tea. "Can you write a letter for me?"

"Write what?"

"A letter. I can read a little. But I can't write."

"Aw, sure, I can do that. In exchange for your tea, of course."

She said she was running late today but would come tomorrow at the same time. She tossed her nearly finished cigarette away. Then, grabbing her sodden clothes, she got up to leave.

"What's your name?"

She gave a nice smile. "Jasmine."

4

On the shore there was a boat café that served cheap meals. It offered overnight accommodation, too. He had his early lunch from the hotel-on-the-water. Afterward he went back to sitting in silence, looking around, focusing on nothing, and thinking nothing. He listened to his surroundings, the sound and soundlessness. The wind hummed. The river rhymed. The sun swanned on the waters.

Bits of conversation from the riverbank, on and off, drifted to his ears. Strikes, shooting, burning, the military—were what they were talking about. Down in the streets of Dhaka, a lot was happening. A lot. He knew.

He kept watching the graces of the river. Canoes carried hyacinths. Steamers came ashore. Loaded and unloaded. Large boats brought groceries, fish, fruits, vegetables. Small boats transported people. Cormorants swam and dove. Pied kingfishers perched and waited for prey.

A lurking smell of human waste loitered along the bank. It mingled with the scent of the river and the odor of the rubbish dumps. There were some people who worked all day. They shed onion and garlic skins. They washed various leaf vegetables—pui sak, palong sak, data sak, pat sak—before sending them to the city markets.

Bathers streamed in at midday to bathe. Then the river, warmed by the sun, became a bustling world. Shouting naked boys played hide-and seek under the water. They stayed long until the water began to penetrate their skin.

Later, the day drowned in the river. The sun bled. Bats took to the sky into the creeping darkness, busying around.

The boat owner studied Shelley when he asked to stay the night. The old man hesitated to take him as one of his poor regulars.

"This is not a single arrangement. You've to share with a stranger." He pointed to his boats.

"I want to sleep undisturbed. I'll pay for two." He paid off the old man.

"Be careful with your wallet. You may get pickpocketed while you sleep." The old man offered him a pillow, gray with grease. Shelley said he was fine. Wearing his pullover, he tucked his slender wallet into his underwear and lay back on the tattered mattress. He looked blankly at the overhead bamboo canopy. He remained still, lost in the language of the water, listening to the gentle waves patting against the boat.

—

Jasmine didn't come the next morning. Shelley waited at the same spot. After breakfast, he returned to his usual spot and kept watching the river. But it seemed that the river flowed dully today. For some time he threw pebbles into the water, to stimulate the river's soul.

He strolled along the bank and came to the spot where he had sacrificed Roxana. He thought of diving into the water and searching for the statue. He murmured Roxana's name a few times, then sighed and plodded along.

The sun was getting hot. Dragonflies darted around gaunt dinghies. He sat to watch the washermen, listening to the cadence of the clothes beating against wooden slabs; as it droned on it turned into a noise. It sounded deafening to him, and the whole place became too gray, too generic. There was too much time to kill. Perhaps he should go to English Road to look for Jasmine and tell her that he was unable to wait until tomorrow. Some months back the senior editor of *Cinemagazine* had asked him if he would be interested in writing a feature article on Kandupatti brothel. Shelley had passed on that, saying the place scared him. Perhaps this was now the right moment. He had all the time in the world.

CHAPTER TWELVE

1

It was around five. The street by Kandupatti looked alive. Flamboyantly dressed girls with overdone makeup were standing outside, by the mouths of the alleys, waiting for customers. A young boy, not more than fifteen, tailed Shelley.

"I can get you a beautiful girl. Very cheap," the boy said.

Shelley regarded the boy. "I'm looking for a girl called Jasmine. Fair skinned." He provided as much description as he could remember of Jasmine. The boy thought for a second and then said to follow him. One or two girls tried to grab Shelley's arm, but the boy barked at them to go away. Passing through a maze of sad and sordid alleys, the boy brought Shelley before a ramshackle room. The door was open. "Jasmine, come out," the boy hollered. A woman in her late twenties peeped out.

"No, no, not her," Shelley quickly said.

The boy then took him to three more women, but to no avail. Afterward, sitting on a bench at a tea stall not far from a garbage dump, Shelley learned that all these Jasmines went to the river in the early morning. As the dark fell, the tea man set up a gas lantern. The boy told Shelley he could get him much better-looking girls than Jasmine.

"It's okay, thanks for your help," Shelley said, sipping his tea.

"Give me another twenty minutes," the boy said, asking Shelley to wait there. He gulped his tea and disappeared into a long, dirty alley. Shelley smoked and noticed that inside the stall some men were drinking.

The tea man looked at him. "You want a shot?"

Shelley shook his head, then out of curiosity asked, "What do you serve here?"

"All kinds."

—

He woke up to the voice of cursing. The distant swearing put him at sea for a moment. A cheap smoke-filled smell hit his nose. Mouth dry and head heavy with a migraine headache, he battled to figure where he was. He peered at the unfamiliar, decrepit low ceiling, full of dicey cracks. Then he made out a woman sitting on the floor. She was combing her hair. He rubbed his eyes. The sights, sounds, and smells—nothing changed. The bed creaked as he moved his leg.

At this the woman turned her head. She grinned. "Up at last?"

Shelley squinted. The face of the woman seemed familiar to him.

"You were at the tea stall last night. Drunk as hell and almost unconscious. Lucky that the boy you hired reached me, so I brought you to my place. How're you feeling now?"

Shelley took some time to get the whole picture. That meant presently he was at the English Road brothel. He looked over the tiny room. The double bed he was on ate up the maximum room space. Touching the bed was a wooden clothing rack, flanked by a three-legged stool and a couple of empty liquor bottles. On the stool, with makeup stuff, a framed mirror leaned back against the wall.

"I'm sorry. I troubled you much," he said to Jasmine.

With a swift stride Jasmine got beside him and put her hand on his forehead. "You have a fever."

"I think I'm good to go now." He attempted to get up while his body chose to refuse.

She gave him a stare. "I know a brothel is a lousy place."

Shelley saw her self-esteem was bigger than her eyes. "I'm sorry. I didn't mean that. I just don't want to trouble you."

"Ah, hell. All men are born to trouble women. Now stop talking and go back to sleep." Then immediately, "Aw, hang on. You need to have your breakfast."

On the bed she put a tin dinner plate and unpacked the food. Two parathas with semolina halwa. Shelley obeyed. But before he could finish one paratha, he belched and ran to the door to vomit.

2

Apart from going to the toilet twice, Shelley spent the day lying in bed, napping and waking every now and then. His temperature went up and down throughout the day. By evening he started to feel better.

Staying in the tiny room, it occurred to him that he could pick up all the sounds of the forbidden place. He heard laughing, shouting, cries of children, drunken voices, a word or two of a song, and whatnot. The brothel never slept. It had countless children in the pit of its womb. During the day the children got boisterous. During the night they strayed around as their mommies slammed the doors in their faces for clients. Or some kids hid under the bed for a brief period, he learned.

The way the people of these red doors talked, Shelley gathered, was by shouting. They referenced sex possibly in every word. And each sentence scarcely finished without a mention of carnal desire. Strangely, Shelley found his ears had already gotten used to it. No longer did their talks sound sordid to him.

At night Jasmine made her bed on the floor. Shelley found it a little hard to go to sleep. From time to time he heard knocking at the closed door or window. To which Jasmine snapped, "Fuck off." One voice stayed a while and urged.

"I'm sick." Jasmine tried to shoo away the voice.

"How many times do you get sick in a month?" grunted the voice.

"Not your business."

Late in the night two drunken Biharis pounded on the door. As the drunken duo wouldn't stop, Jasmine half opened the door. Shelley watched the two men, having poor balance, begging Jasmine to let them in. She explained the fact in every possible way. They begged her even more. They said they loved her. They were happy to marry her straightaway. When Jasmine attempted to shut the door, one forced himself in, shoving her aside.

"We two gonna sleep with you, Jass. Kick this Bengali ass out of here. Nowww," The mouse-faced one demanded in his slurred speech.

"Go away. Go fuck your mother," Jasmine's stern voice boomed out.

"Oi! Who do you think you are, bitch?" The other ranted. "Not even a dog will fuck a bitch like you."

So began a real rumpus. Shelley tried to stay mild mannered. But the moment the mouse-faced one pulled her sari, Shelley leaped out of the bed and threw a jab right into his face. The drunkard lost balance and fell. The other drunkard stepped up to attack. Jasmine stood in between them and shouted for help. A girl from next door rushed in. Shortly, with a lathi bamboo stick in hand, one tall, remarkably fleshy man hulked into the scene. He caught the two Biharis by the back of their necks, like geese, and dragged them out. Not from the room but from the zone. From the distance their swearing rang out. The drunk-ards yelled that they would see Shelley in hell.

Jasmine shut the door and then checked on Shelley to see if he was hurt. He was not.

"Why did you do that?" she snapped. "This always happens here."

"The filthy bastards—" he sputtered and clenched his fist. "Wish I could kill them."

"What do you think I am? Look at me. I am just a filthy piece of meat."

"Oh, really?"

"Why did you take this risk for me? They're not good folks."

"Don't worry about me. I'm not afraid of death."

"But I do worry for you."

"All right then. I'll leave. You go on with your business. That makes you happy?"

Jasmine stared, still and speechless. Tearful. "I earn more than I need. You get better. Then leave. That'll make me happy."

"No."

"Just stay tonight."

3

Shelley opened his eyes from a soft touch on the forehead. He found Jasmine feeling his temperature. The window was open, and it was dawn outside. He smelled the cool air.

"Don't you ever sleep?" he asked.

Jasmine did not reply. In the half-dark or half-light of the room, he could make out her smile.

"The sun will be up shortly," she said, pulling a dress from the cloth-ing rack. "Can you turn around for a minute? I gotta change to pray."

He did so.

After changing Jasmine opened the door and performed her ablutions on the threshold. Then she closed the door, covered herself with a long scarf, and stepped on her prayer mat facing west. Prayer over, she switched on the light and took out a book from a small tin trunk. In a honeyed, cooing voice she read it for about twenty minutes. Before putting the Quran back into its place, Jasmine stepped up to him and blew her breath over his body.

"People think we shouldn't have the right to practice religion," she said.

"That's ridiculous." He wished the holy breath she'd put on him could do a miracle.

"I shouldn't be punished for the life I haven't chosen. When there's no way out."

There is always a way out, he wanted to say. But he didn't, because for a girl like Jasmine, society could not have her back.

"You Hindu, na?" Jasmine asked.

Lightly, he sat up. "Well, I was born in a Hindu family. But how did you—"

"Of course, I didn't check your thing." Jasmine broke into a soft laugh like the soft, dawning daylight. "Have a guess."

He gave up guessing.

"When you were delirious, you were asking for jal," she said.

"Oh."

His family, like numerous Hindu Bengalis, used *jal* for water whereas the Muslims used *paani*. Although he was comfortable using *paani*, maybe *jal* came out of his mouth without his knowledge.

"The first person who translated the Quran into Bengali was a Hindu," he said after a silence. "You know that?"

Open-mouthed, Jasmine expressed her ignorance. A moment later she asked, "You got no family?"

He glanced at her and sighed. "Once upon a time I did. This country got us all butchered."

"A-all? How? Riots?"

He nodded, looking the other way. She pestered him for details, but he remained unresponsive. When he turned to her, she was in tears.

She sat on the corner of the bed and wiped her eyes. Her father had died before she was born, Jasmine began. Her eldest brother eventually filled up that space. He was nine years older than her. He worked for the Adamjee Jute Mills. When the riot occurred between Bengalis and Biharis in 1954, he was killed. His dead body was never found.

"If he were alive," she sniffled, "I wouldn't be here today." She sat motionless. Tears trickled down her cheeks. "You," said Jasmine in a sudden and warm utterance, "remind me of my brother. When I first saw you, I thought perhaps my brother had never died."

Shelley surveyed her flickering eyes as she spoke. Outside she wore the skin of a slut, but inside she carried the soul of a sister. He thought of his elder sister. One winter, he remembered he had fallen sick with a cough and fever. Mother employed his sister to pour water over his head when his body temperature increased. For a week he couldn't eat. His sister said, running her fingers through his hair, "There's no fun without you. Get well soon, brother. From now, you can have the bigger portion of the omelet." The two always fought over almost everything, from meals to study materials. During breakfast, the regular squabble was over onion omelets. Shelley sighed. His eyelids fluttered. He had almost forgotten her touch, even her punches on his back. It would be five years come July since his ma and his sisters had left.

"How did you end up here, may I ask?" he asked Jasmine.

"I was married off at twelve. Few months after my marriage, my husband brought me here to see his aunt. I hadn't the foggiest idea about his intentions. He left selling me to his so-called aunt, who was a procurer."

"Are you in touch with your family"

"Family?" she snorted. "They spit on me. They don't want me near their lives. But they love the money I send."

Silence invaded the room.

"What was that letter about?" he asked a little later. "That you wanted me to write earlier?"

"I just made that up to talk to you." A small smile tugged at her lips.

Out of the blue, bristling shouts in the Dhakaiya colloquial dialect spilled out somewhere, breaking the early morning into a million pieces. Jasmine got up to fetch breakfast.

CHAPTER THIRTEEN

1

At the railway ticket counter, Shelley discovered some money in his kurta's pocket, which was certainly not his. Jasmine must have slipped it into his pocket. Such an amount in his current state was enough to last more than a few weeks. He wondered for a while if he should head back to return the money. But the love he found in his pocket and the happiness he pictured on her face were worth more than the return.

Shelley caught a train that carried him away from the city. Walking out of the station, he wandered the narrow street for a while. A tin sign arrested his attention.

Shukkoor Hotel
Low-cost accommodation

He stepped into the unsightly roadside hotel. It turned out to be fabulously inexpensive. In the guest register he changed his name.

"Name please?" the receptionist asked.

"Se-selim," he stammered.

"Selim . . . ?" the staff looked up, waiting to hear the rest.

"Selim Sarkar," he replied fast.

A dingy corridor led him to an unswept room. At the sound of the door opening, two cockroaches, seemingly a couple, scurried under the bed. He exhaled. The only earthly creatures he was scared of—and sick of—were cockroaches. Their flying especially gave him goose bumps. Roxana used to make fun of him. She was so bold that she could hold cockroaches in her hands. The best way to cure his cockroach phobia, she once told him, was to make him live with them. She was right. When he was kept in custody for a day, he had to lie down alongside these roaches. And there, his fear had dissipated. He had to let it go.

He didn't tell the receptionist to get rid of the cockroaches when he headed out for lunch.

Back at the Shukkoor Hotel, he popped into the communal bathroom. All four corners and the ceiling were rife with cobwebs. The bubbling and peeling walls were scrawled with raunchy graffiti. Shelley felt claustrophobic. The forceful stench of ammonia was powerful enough to suffocate someone in minutes. Right after urination, he pulled the door open hard and sprang into his room for some breathable oxygen. He gasped for unsullied air, though the room was musty and stuffy. He seated himself. The bed, at the slightest movement, moaned and screamed with pain. And the rickety stool was tormented by the weight of a half-empty water jug. He smoked one cigarette after another to make the room air breathable, livable.

He heard his neighbor humming a popular Bangla movie song. Outside, the last light of the sun was waning. He sprawled on the bed like a silent shadow. He looked to his left. He wished Roxana were here next to his bed. He thought of Maya. He should have said goodbye to her before leaving the city. It had been a month and a half since he was last in touch with her. He wondered if he would see her again in this life.

The room was moon filled. He tried to sleep.

2

He awoke to the sound of birds. The day was breaking. Fresh, green-scented cool air pervaded the room. He inhaled deeply. Maybe, Shelley thought, if he set off for Dhaka and went home, he would find Roxana waiting for him there. Like nothing had happened and everything was a mere nightmare. He sighed and lit a cigarette.

Across the road there was a café outside the hotel. Shelley had a large breakfast. After tea, he strolled down along the highway. He liked the quaint breeze around him. It smelled of mud, of dung, and of soft land. The winter sun felt warm by the time he was treading a dirt road after leaving the tarmac.

By the roadside a small crowd was enjoying music. Two Baul singers were playing. The mystic song the duo was singing, Shelley had heard countless times. Nonetheless, this time it hit him hard and took him far away. The simple yet significant lyrics brought tears to his eyes.

With long tulsi neck beads, the Bauls were in saffron robes. Both of them had long hair with day-old stubble. They were in their late thirties. Their instruments were mismatched, though—one played a single-string ektara and the other a double-string dotara.

Long after the crowd broke up, Shelley stayed behind. He tagged along with the duo. He asked if he could join their musical group. He could run errands for them. They said they had no group; they simply traveled about singing. They said he looked lost, and this shouldn't be the right path for him. Still, if he genuinely loved music, he was welcome to join them.

"Why do you Bauls always travel?" Shelley asked.

The ektara Baul laughed mutely. "That's our worship. That's how we meet God."

"God? Where is He?"

"Where is He?" The ektara Baul roared, rocking his body. "He is right before me. I am talking to Him now."

Shelley was speechless for a minute. He asked if they could teach him to sing.

Both the Bauls guffawed at this. The reply came from the dotara Baul. "Who taught the birds to sing? Music can't be taught. It has to be learned."

The Bauls were heading to Dhaka. Shelley eventually learned that both of them were married with children. Other than the monsoon season, they traveled all year round. The ektara Baul was a fourth-generation Baul singer. His parents, his siblings, even his wife could sing. The dotara Baul, on the other hand, was Muslim and did not come from a singing family. Childhood friends, the two Bauls had grown up in the same hamlet.

Later on the Bauls busked at a bazaar. There, singing for a restaurant owner, they received a free lunch. For being a Baul associate Shelley enjoyed a meal, too. Before sundown they had two more performances.

The Bauls stopped at a large field, under a rain tree. A grocery store across the road had lent them a kerosene lantern. Their sleeping arrangements had also been made in its storage area. As the sky turned ash-black, folks set to gather under the tree. The ektara Baul started off with a famous folk song about love.

Out of love a death
Never dies, never drowns in water . . .

The evening of music ended late at night. At ease, the Bauls then sat down to prepare the chillum pipe. From the audience a handful stayed behind to enjoy the ganja smoke. Shelley couldn't refuse. The sensation was intense. Time began to melt away. He asked the dotara Baul to sing him the Lalon song he liked the most. The dotara Baul sang.

I haven't seen my neighbor even for a day
Who lives near my house in a city of mirrors
A sea of water surrounds the city
And I have no boat to cross it.
I long to see her
But how can I reach her place?
How can I describe my neighbor?
She has no hands, no feet, no shoulders, no head
Sometimes she floats up in the air
Sometimes deep in the water
If that neighbor touched me once
All my sufferings, death pains would go away
She and Lalon live in the same place
Yet their worlds are worlds apart.

Each and every word of the song struck Shelley harder than ever. Hands behind his head, he lay flat on his back. He cried. A flood of tears streamed down his cheeks, flooded his ears, flooded the green grass, and flooded the earth. And his body bobbed up and down in the floodwater.

—

Shelley awoke feeling cold and dizzy. It took some time to gather where he was. In the solitude of the storeroom, he was all alone. The sun slipped into the room, penetrating the weathered window. He pushed himself up.

The grocer said the Bauls had gone to a private house to sing. Shelley had been so dead to the world that they did not wake him. The grocer told him how to get to the house where the duo had gone. Shelley half listened. He asked for a packet of biscuits to calm his growling stomach.

3

Shelley watched the western sky; the dying scent of the saffron sun captivated him. And he thought—the thought he had gone through infinite times. That evening, if he hadn't passed through SM Hall, he would have a different life now. Life was so unpredictable, like the weather. You could not be certain of your next step, could not be sure of the pit your foot would plunge into the next minute. Bad luck. Misfortune. Why did they always chase him? Wouldn't it have been way better if the police had gunned him down rather than King Siraj?

Having left the Bauls, Shelley traveled to Narayanganj. Brass bell chimes broke out as he entered the Lokenath Ashram in Barodi. He had long wanted to visit this place. The cadence of chimes was weird and wonderful. It gave mixed feelings at different parts of the day. The dawn chimes sounded blissful, the evening chimes sorrowful. Yet the bells and the chimes were always the same in the temples.

Here in Barodi, on the outskirts of Dhaka, after traveling the world on foot, the saint Lokenath had finally settled down. Shelley stood before the tomb of the saint, pondering his fifty-year-long frosty meditation in the Himalayas without clothes.

Shelley received a free meal, and afterward he found a spot in the visitors' shed to sleep. Many visitors there had come from distant places. He overheard one talking about the miracles of Baba Lokenath. Shelley buried his body under his woolen shawl and drifted off.

The ashram activities began before daybreak, with regular brass bell chimes and kirtan song thereafter. Shelley lay still and listened to it. Much later he was sitting on the edge of the pond in the morning sun when he heard his name. Before him, down by the water, he saw a man looking at him; the homely face had a few smallpox marks. He was carrying a bamboo basket, loaded with vegetables he'd just washed.

"Minto!" cried Shelley.

Minto came up and gave Shelley a warm, shaky embrace. "Give me a second, I'll be right back." Minto lifted the bamboo basket and headed for the kitchen area. When he returned, Shelley noticed that his childhood friend had already started losing hair.

Minto had gone to the same village school as Shelley. The summer they were in eighth grade, Minto and his family left for India. Without telling anyone, they disappeared from Gopala one night. Minto's elder brother had sold everything in secret, Shelley later learned from his father.

"You haven't changed at all," Minto said.

Shelley smiled.

"Did you stay here last night?" Minto asked.

"Yeah. At the visitors' shed."

"Ah. That's why you look terrible. It must be cold in there."

"Yes, a little."

"I could have arranged something better if I'd known."

"Never mind. What do you do here?"

"Not much. A poor servant of Baba. A voluntary worker."

Minto had been at the ashram for six months. He grilled Shelley about Gopala, about the home they'd left behind. Their unmatched mango grove. Their aged date palm tree that produced the sweetest juice in the entire village. Their pond and many other little things.

"It's not life there," Minto said of his past life as a refugee in Kolkata. "They call us 'Bangal.' Just like calling us names."

Upon leaving Gopala, Minto said, their tragedy had really begun at the border. Although they had hired a dealer to cross it, they were betrayed by the East Pakistan border security, who literally robbed them. In the name of a body search, they were only just spared the indignity of his mother and sister being forced to strip. And by the time they were in Kolkata, they were down and out. The few relatives they had there never helped. His mother's sister didn't even open the door to say hello. They managed to land in a refugee camp, but it was too late. Minto sighed, and his hollow voice ceased for a while.

"How's your mother?" Shelley asked.

"Happy in heaven. She died of cholera. It was a kind of survival, actually."

"Your sister?"

"Whoring around. That's the respectable job destitute refugee girls can get."

"Your brother? What does he do?"

Minto sniggered. "Drinking and gambling."

Shelley decided not to ask any more and not to tell Minto that his own mother and sisters had also moved to India. His mother's brother took good care of them, so they had done better there than many others.

"When we were in Gopala, at least we had food and never starved," Minto said, as though he were complaining. But Kolkata had given them a taste of hunger. His mother's dying wish had been to eat ilish fish. This East Bengal fish from the Padma River was a big luxury in West Bengal. The price was beyond the purse of any refugee.

Minto returned alone. There was no point dying in a foreign land, he said. "If necessary, I'm happy to get circumcised to live here. After all, this is my birthland." He broke off. "What does it matter being a Hindu or Muslim? My skin will be same anyway. As Lalon said in his song, at times of arrival or departure, what sign of religion do you bear?"

Shelley listened to his friend in silence. He thought of his baba in Gopala.

4

After a midday meal they set out for the bazaar, as Minto needed to get some groceries for the ashram. With farmland on both sides they walked down the road, the artistic landscape all around.

"I like this place," said Minto. "This ashram, the incredible river. Down there is a nice little old city, Sonargaon. What else does a soul need to be happy?"

"So you're happy here?" Shelley said.

"I am. Even though I have nothing of my own. But I am happy."

From the riverbank Minto hired a boat. Climbing on the boat, Minto took out a folded newspaper page from his pajama pocket. He unfolded the single page and handed it to Shelley.

"Read this." He pointed to an article.

The article, an opinion piece, was published the previous day, dated February 1, 1969. The writer held the position of a principal of a college. Shelley looked over the sentences in bold type first:

> *I do not know where Bangladesh is. Or East Bengal. Is it an independent country? Are we not the citizens of Pakistan? A state for the Muslims? Then why lately are some voices bringing up the word Bangladesh? We have to remember Hindus did not want this land. They never did and never will. We always should be alert about that. About their*

conspiracy to break this country. And, sadly, Bangla language and culture are the means of their conspiracy. Therefore, the Muslims of Pakistan should use one language to stay united. That is Urdu. For the sake of Pakistan's unity, why not place greater importance on Urdu, the sweetest language to my knowledge.

Shelley returned the page after reading.

"This thing disgusts me," Minto said. "There in India, they also do the same thing, fuck Pakistan all the time. Here, they fuck India all the time. It's nauseating." He paused for a few seconds. "That's why I'm at the ashram."

Shelley appreciated Minto's choice. He told him how protesters were being killed in Dhaka, almost every day. The situation was fiercely sickening up there. So he had come here for a breath of fresh air.

Shelley looked up at the sky, cloudless, brilliantly blue. A water-scented wind swept over him, freshened his face. Halfway up the river, a slice of island came into sight. As the boat slid through the water, the island seemed to have been planted there a little while ago. In the close distance the island became more visible.

"What is that?" Shelley asked. "Is that where we're landing?"

Minto chuckled. "That's a char land. No one lives there. We go farther down."

The boat now glided alongside the char island. The boatman said there were some new islands, land accretion, in this river. But this particular one was uncaptured and deserted. For the presence of ghosts and fairies. Spiritual bodies always preferred silence, preferred nature, he explained. Last year someone had been brave enough to try farming there, and within two weeks his dead body was found floating in the river. And before that another unafraid soul had gone to live there and ended up becoming insane.

"But the island is very fertile," Minto butted in. "New islands are like virgin girls, you know."

Shelley had never taken a boat ride in this river before, but the new island looked very familiar to him, as if he knew every inch of it and could walk around on it blindfolded.

—

It was market day, and the store in the bazaar was somewhat packed. Shelley found a day-old newspaper at the counter and looked for reports regarding KK's murder. The paper was full of protest news, and he learned that the six-point movement had now turned into an eleven-point demand. The editorial page opined that the Agartala Conspiracy Case was now a big mess, and the government had fallen into their own trap.

Shelley remained quiet on their way to the ashram. In the evening, after light supper, he sat by the pond with Minto. They spent about an hour talking about their village and reminiscing their happy school days.

Minto arranged Shelley's bed in the ashram's guest cottage.

5

Shelley woke up from a dream. In his dream, he was wandering alone on the virgin island. The images of the island were still so fresh in his mind that he felt he knew the place like a book. After the sandy shore there was gorgeous green grass, then two lofty rain trees, then a line of long reeds . . .

When the sun was up, Minto came with two cups of milk tea. While they chatted, he thought of asking Minto to get him a job at the ashram.

Maybe he could do the paperwork here. All he wanted in return was food and a place to sleep. Then it occurred to him that it might rouse suspicions.

Before leaving, Minto said he would bring Shelley's breakfast. Later someone entered carrying a thali plate, with a few luchis and sabji in it. The man said that Minto had gotten busy with the ashram work.

Shelley ate sitting in the sun on the veranda. He noticed, among some wandering visitors near the peepal tree, a family with two kids. He remembered, many years ago when he was a boy, he visited the local temple in Gopala with his family. It was during a Durga Puja festival. Baba, though he was not much interested in godly matters, accompanied them as well. Shelley and his sisters had Baba buy them jilapi sweets from the shop outside.

Shelley sighed. He lit a cigarette and got up to take a stroll. Outside the ashram, everything was still damp, bathed in dew. He walked down to the river. A man passed him, a wooden plow over his shoulder. Next to a roadside tea shop, three people were sitting around a fire. Under a banyan tree by the bank, Shelley saw a litter of puppies frolicking in the sunlight. The stray mother dog was away. The puppies looked three weeks old. Seven of them, one white, two black, and the rest were fawn colored.

The white pup ascended a pile of firewood nearby. Its head moved back and forth, legs wobbled. Climbing a fraction up, it paused and peered down at his siblings. Front legs forward, it carefully crawled up to descend, lowered itself onto the wood below, but ceased and quickly crawled back. Its two beady eyes then searched for its mother. Not finding her anywhere, it started to whimper.

"Just come down," Shelley said to the pup. "It's easy."

The pup looked up at him, squeaked, and wagged its tail. Shelley reached the woodpile and lifted the pup. Its body was warm, soft, silky.

In his palms it squeaked and moved its paws in the air. Shortly afterward, the mother came along, barking. He put down the pup. But the warmth of its softness lingered in his hands.

He gazed at the river. Across the horizon the far-off river looked like another world, mating with the azure skies. A boatman asked him if he needed a ride. Shelley said yes and got aboard. The wind whistled. Clean, crisp air chilled him. When the boat set to sail alongside the virgin island, Shelley spoke.

"Take me to that island."

The boatman, arched with age, had sunburned cheeks with deep wrinkles. His jaundiced eyes squinted as if he didn't understand him.

"Take me to the char island," Shelley repeated.

"Are you not going to the bazaar?"

"No."

"Are you mad?" The boatman stared at him, nonplussed. "That place is full of ghosts."

"Take me there," he said.

6

The sprawling virgin island was charmingly green, isolated, and satisfyingly humanless. Surrounded by river, the land had bottomless blue above and boundless green beneath. Under his feet Shelley felt the luscious landscape, tender grass glinting in the soft sunshine. A tantalizing kingdom unmoored from human touch. The verdant vastness pleased his eyes. Numberless herons and cormorants were lounging around. Some curiously looked at Shelley.

A sweet breeze gently licked his face, stirred his hair. Here the scent of the river was refreshing. He listened to the sound of small waves. He smelled the rich blend of fresh vegetation. A flight of birds shrieked overhead. In the distance a couple of boats were floating down. "What a wonderful land," he shouted.

Along the soft river's edge he walked. He felt music around in everything. The low-lying new char island was about a quarter mile square. During the rainy season a good part of the land, perhaps, would go under water. Here and there several copses of coconut trees turned the island into a beautiful painting. Up ahead he found an egg-shaped water body. A sizable pond. In the middle of the island, that pond connected to the river through a serpentine route. But what were those on the water moving? Ducks?

Shelley marveled at the crystalline pond water and its sporting swimmers. They were chokha-chokhi ducks, he said to himself. The beautiful honey-colored waterfowls were eying Shelley. He stood rooted. He remembered going once with Baba to a winter wetland to see these ducks. Also called Brahminy ducks, they paired for life, Baba told him. Paired for life! Shelley murmured. Inside the kans grass by the pond, he spotted more ducks. A team of ducks in fact.

With light steps he came to the fringe of the pond. Dropped his clothes and got into the water, being careful not to scare the creatures. The swimming ducks kept enough distance from him. Soon they seemed to get used to his presence. Shelley washed his body. He dove. He swam. He floated. On moonlit nights this should be quite a place for fairies to bathe, he thought.

When he got out of the water, he felt that he had become a part of the island. He looked around. Everywhere it was green land. Then the river. Then nothing was visible. He didn't put his clothes on. With all his nakedness he felt pure. He reached the other edge of the island. Stood on the muddy bank. The peaceful river splashed against the bank and washed his feet. Cool and nice it felt. He watched the tidal current for a long time. It was on the go. It was going in one direction, and the current would come back in the opposite direction. There was a constant coming and going. Four times a day. River sought the sea, life did death, he told himself.

He tried to remember when he had last had a river bath. All he could remember were his childhood days. On the way home from school, with other boys, he used to bathe naked in the river. Then he would sunbathe to dry his sand-coated skin before putting on his clothes.

Beneath the white sun, the shimmering waters of Shitalakhya were glistening and sparkling in every direction. Shelley jumped into the river.

—

The first thing Shelley saw, opening his eyes, was a monitor lizard. Just ten feet away, it was staring at him, flicking its forked tongue in and out. It tuned and headed down to the shrubs of kans grass as he stared back.

He was resting against a tree trunk. As he stretched out, his arms ached from all the swimming. He felt exhausted and hungry. Since he had disembarked on this island, he had only drunk water. He lay flat on his back. Then he started rolling around in the grass. Under the mellow sun his bare body delighted in its ticklish touch. Like a light feather, he felt like he was gliding through the air.

The late afternoon light began to fade. Shelley slipped into his clothes. As he strolled along the bank, a dinghy came into view. But the boat was so far away, and because the boatman's back was to him, it was pointless trying to draw his attention. Before the sun went down, he must get out of here.

About half an hour later, standing at another point, he saw a houseboat on the horizon, sailing westward. He yelled at the top of his voice.

He waved his arms madly overhead. But the boat steadily sailed past the island into the sinking sun. The sky was tinged with pink and purple and red. The wind was eastward, he gathered, so his voice didn't reach the boatman.

The cries of the birds were loud. The daylight was dying fast. His hunger had died down. Perhaps he should start collecting dry twigs to make a fire. It occurred to him that it would be a full moon tonight. But a thought was beating inside him. What if the virgin island was really haunted? He didn't believe in ghosts anyway. And he had nothing to gain or lose. Maybe this was the night he would figure this mystery out.

He dragged two fallen coconut leaves to the feet of two trees and built a little shelter. He made a staff out of a branch. He collected stray twigs with leaves for firewood in case it got cold at night.

The big moon rose. Outside his shelter, he sat facing the river. He listened to the screaming of crickets. He could live here, he reflected. He could reign here. Growing food here would be no big deal. This was the place he could have brought Roxana to live an undisturbed life. In fact, he should have brought King Siraj and Laloo here, too, and they all could have lived a happy life, much safer than in the civilized world.

Shelley carefully took out Roxana's letter from his wallet. The words glowed under the bright moon. He closed his eyes. Images came alive. He saw Roxana. He remembered her dreamy grin, when many years ago he plucked boroi jujube from Motla's for her. He heard her muffled voice, her subdued laughter. He smelled a faint scent of jasmine—the odor of her skin. Then everything went black.

An excruciating emptiness smoldered in the pit of his chest. A lump welled up in his throat. A salty taste saturated his mouth. The world around him blurred. Tears pooled in his eyes. His nose snuffled. He buried his face between his knees. He didn't know how long he'd remained like this. All at once he heard a sound—the sound of someone walking in the water. His heart stopped. Eyes popped out. A human figure, a woman, emerged from the riverbank and headed toward him. He was trembling, violently and uncontrollably. Then it appeared to him that he knew the woman. In the moonlight her face was luminous, clear as in the daylight. Her gentle steps ceased before him.

7

"It's me," said the voice, intimate.

To him the voice was unmistakable. "Roxana!"

"Tell me. Can you see me?"

"Yeah."

"Can you feel me?" She extended her hand to him.

Shelley felt her hand. The same slender and delicate hand.

On her face appeared a dimpled smile. Roxana stepped to him, took his hands in hers. And she looked deep into his eyes.

"Life lives in the present. Free from fear. Open your heart." Her voice was soft but firm. "Give me a good hug, hon. I am hungry for your arms around me."

He had his arms around her, held her tight against him. Warm and delicate, her skin was like the petals of a hibiscus on a sunny day. She was wearing the amber jamdani muslin he had bought her from New Market, the same sari she had worn on the morning when the police arrested them. Her ankle-long tresses were pulled back in a messy bun, the same messy bun she had worn that day. He hugged her till he could feel himself no more.

"I couldn't leave with my unfulfilled desires. Leaving our marriage unconsummated," she said.

A queer wind blew. And aloud the foliage of the trees fluttered. Words failed him. Hand in hand, they came into the open space. The cool night air caressed his face, her face.

She smiled a secret smile. "I'll give you the finest night ever."

She ran her fingers through his hair. Stroked his face. Nuzzled his neck. Drizzled him with kisses. He kissed her back. Sucked her lips. Tasted her warm tongue. Licked her earlobes.

"Undress me," she said. Her sultry face had the red of silk cotton-tree flowers.

He pulled off the sari from her shoulders and let the free end slide down. Now she was in her short silk blouse, baring her midriff and majestic curves.

"Know what? I feel like dancing." Her voice trembled with excitement.

In the air she let her hands flutter twice, and she started dancing. Her rhythmic movement was spontaneous, natural. She pulled him toward her, to dance with her. The large grassy ground turned into an epic dance floor. They danced as they felt. They whirled as their souls swung to the music of crickets.

The joy was immense.

She nestled her head on his shoulder, hugging him. His heart could hear hers. Over his neck, her breathing was brisk, lewd. She removed his clothes. And he hers, the rest of it.

Roxana let her hair down. Her long hair unrolled, spilled over her back. He watched. Her naked anatomy. The naturalness of her body. Her bewitching bosom. Her magnificent thighs. Her sensuous buttocks. The scent of her body changed. She smelled different when she was turned on.

He touched, tasted her everywhere. His tongue mated with her tongue, sucking the whole sea. Her armpits were aromatic, and her virginal yoni spicy. Bit by bit he drank of her feverish, dripping body. Drank her deathless beauty.

From nowhere a flock of fireflies appeared. The night glowed. The ground glittered. Bathing in the warm light of fireflies, he saw the grassy ground turning into a bed of bliss. His breath burned her. And hers his. He entered her. She entered him. And they became one. The pleasure seemed to be eternal. All the past was dead. All the future was dead. Alive now was the present. Together, they went into an intoxicating, sweet slumber.

—

Much, much later, Roxana awoke Shelley from the pleasure sleep.

"It's time," she said. "I need to leave."

Shelley wrinkled his forehead.

She gave him a knowing look. "Yes, officially I'm not here. Part of me is still here, but part of me is over there."

Her voice so surreal, poetic, he could keep hearing it. Looking into her magical eyes, he knew everything that he should know. Roxana had been partitioned between this life and the other.

"Why go, Roxana? Stay."

She gave a sweet smile.

"Oh, Roxana! Take me with you!"

"No. You stay here. I'm happy you're here to breathe for me."

Shelley found no breathable air to inhale. He cried, "Do you really need to go?"

"Sing me a lullaby," she demanded.

He caressed her hair and crooned:

Children fall asleep
Silence sets in

The Bargis come to our lands
Birds have eaten the grains
How shall I pay the rent? . . .

He kissed her for the last time. She kissed him back. He did feel like a father giving a goodnight kiss to his daughter.

"Sweet dreams," he told her.

"I am you. I always was. Always shall be."

"I can't feel myself."

"There is no self. We are one."

She released his hand and made for the river. He stood still. He heard her footsteps wading into the water. She didn't look back. Her figure gradually dwindled, faded to a dot on the horizon.

Birds began chirping. Morning twilight obscured the moon's brightness. Soon it started raining. Light rain. The drizzle-like drops drenched him. He didn't move.

At daybreak he saw a fishing boat appear on the horizon where Roxana had disappeared. The boat seemed to sail toward the island. He waved his hands.

CHAPTER FOURTEEN

1

A protest march was passing through Johnson Road, heading toward Bangla Bazaar. Shelley was walking along the pavement. It was hot. But he didn't remove his woolen shawl, which draped over his shoulders. His eyes were on the ground. Yet he could sense the police van in the near distance. Were they watching him? He didn't dare to check. Making eye contact with the police was dangerous. Somehow they resented such boldness in civilians. They preferred to maintain a sort of "king to his subjects" distance.

A hand came down on his shoulder, and a voice hissed, "You! Finally!"

It was Fourqan. "We thought you—" he gulped and glanced over his shoulder.

"What, me?"

"Let's go to the park."

They crossed the road. Shelley looked about the sidewalk. He had always seen a parrot fortune teller sitting by the road of the park. Where was he today? Countless days Shelley had strolled past the astrologer parrot, never feeling an urge to have his fortune told. But today he longed to hear about his future.

"I was out getting some groceries," Fourqan said once they were in Victoria Park. "Instead I caught up with the protest march. Lucky I did."

Shelley scratched his beard, cleared his throat.

"Why are you wandering around like Ibn Battuta?" Fourqan dropped the sneer from his voice. "Think your beard is good enough as a disguise?"

"I'm not trying to hide."

"What then? Trying to be a badass?"

He did not answer.

"You're a class-A crazy. You know that?" Fourqan said. "Sure, people are having hard times here. The police are too busy to tackle the protesters. They're panicky. The fall of the dictator is just a matter of time. But whatever happens, you shouldn't take the risk. You could get caught at any moment."

"I know."

"Then get away to India. As soon as possible. What're you waiting for? We thought you'd gone already." Fourqan then went on to describe the recent killings during the protests. People in other major cities were also getting rowdy. How long would it be? How long could the dictator survive?

Perhaps the best thing the field marshal could do, thought Shelley, was to find a copy of Shakespeare's *Macbeth*. If he was too busy to read the whole tragedy, he could look at the final scene. And then go play the Roman Fool.

"Tell me," Fourqan whispered, "how did you do it?"

Shelley glanced up quizzically. "What?"

"Well, er . . . finishing that bastard."

He watched a shalik bird walk in the grass.

"Seriously. You turned into a hero." Fourqan beamed with pleasure. Then touched his arm firmly. "We're proud of you. The great thing is

NSF leaders are shitting and pooping in their pants now. All gone into hiding."

The shalik pecked in the grass. It leaped into the air shortly and flew away with an earthworm curled up in its yellow beak.

Shelley started picking at his nails and twitched his legs.

"Where have you been hiding, may I ask?"

"I'm not hiding. I'm traveling."

"Okay. If you need anything, say, money or clean clothes, you know, I'm always here for you."

"How is Manick?" Shelley asked.

"Manick? A spineless jellyfish! Left for India yesterday."

"What?"

"To settle his family back in Kolkata. Sounds ridiculous, right? He was looking for you everywhere. As we all were." Fourqan raised his shoulders. "Manick will be back in three weeks anyway."

For a long moment Victoria Park reverberated with the roaring of a protest march in the road. Shelley felt his ears ring. He coughed and cleared his phlegmy throat.

"Hey, you okay?"

Shelley nodded. "Just a cold."

Fourqan asked again about his whereabouts and his plans. Shelley didn't reply. He slowly rose and said he might go to his place tonight.

—

Shelley walked fast, walked carelessly through different alleys. His head felt light. He felt like he was swimming through the streets. At some point, he found himself before Dream Garden. The entrance was clustered all over with dead Rangoon creeper. There was no sound around. The wooden gate in the late afternoon looked strange. A large padlock was hanging from the rusty metal rings. Had he come yesterday, he could have seen Maya. He touched the gate and curled his fingers into a fist. He felt an excruciating cry piercing his heart. He turned and started walking. A few seconds later he halted and looked back. He gazed up at the roof. Perhaps if he waited a while, he could catch a glimpse of Maya there?

He staggered to his feet and thought of his own place—already forsaken by him. The rotted wooden gate there must be worn out, carrying the weight of a discolored padlock around its neck.

2

After two months Shelley set to write to his father. Though, putting pen to paper, he found nothing to write about. A phrase from his father flashed across his mind: *An aimless man is a wandering lunatic.* He wanted to write that he had decided to end this Sisyphean life. But it would be too much to bear for Baba.

To pay for the postage Shelley discovered he had very little money left. He sighed and told himself he didn't need money anymore. Walking away from the post office, he headed off to see Inspector Mahmood Zaman.

—

Reeking of cigarette smoke, the fuggy room of the inspector looked exactly the same as the last time. The same humongous desk awash with files had the same name plate that read "Inspector Mahmood Zaman." Sitting behind the desk was the same inspector. And the same portrait hung above his head—the creator of the country. The only change was a new tin ashtray that sat before him on the right side of the desk.

The inspector shot Shelley a look, sipped from his cracked teacup, and asked, "Yes?"

"Umm." Shelley took a breath.

"Yes? How can I help?"

"My name is Shelley Majumder. I killed KK."

The inspector's eyes under his bushy eyebrows squinted. His cup, clamped between his fingers, was suspended in the air. He put the cup down, and his fingers clicked, motioning for Shelley to sit.

Shelley sat in the chair on the right.

"Are you not the guy . . ." Inspector Mahmood Zaman pointed his finger at him, as if trying to remove Shelley's beard in his mind, "we caught . . . because you ran away with a girl?"

Shelley nodded.

At this another policeman entered and left a letter on the desk. The inspector took it, and before he finished skimming the message, the telephone rang. He said hello and then suddenly straightened. "Yessir, yessir," "nosir, nosir," and "okaysir, okaysir," his mouth kept producing. As if the caller on the other end were right here watching him, with a cane in his hand.

The inspector put down the receiver and exhaled deeply. He thought for a moment. "Right." The inspector turned to Shelley. "What do you want me to do?"

"I don't know," said Shelley. "I'm a criminal, I guess."

The inspector gave him a skewering stare. "Look. We're way too busy to deal with this at the moment. That NSF KK? He was a yucky bastard. Everyone knows that. We're not the least bothered about his murder. The whole country is out on the street now. Protesting day and night. I can arrest you for sure. But I reckon the angry mob will just demand your release."

Shelley could certainly see the inspector was having a turbulent time. Eyes heavy from sleep deprivation, the police's face was unshaved, and he smelled of sweat.

The inspector let out another gust of wind through his lips. "Look, take my advice." His voice now a whisper. "Get out of this place and move straight to India. Never look back."

Shelley met his gaze. For a moment he walked down memory lane, replaying the last minutes he'd been with Roxana. He felt Roxana's presence beside him.

"No," he said.

"What do you mean 'no'? You're young. Go and start a fresh life over there."

Life? What life? Shelley wondered. The mentioning of his "fresh life" made him think of Roxana's resting place. He sat silent for a long moment. Then he sighed, got up, and slowly left the room.

THE END

ACKNOWLEDGMENTS

I would like to thank Jon Cook, River Stillwood, Murtala Ramat, Rafee Shaams, Tasnuva Nuzhat, Steve Trelogan, Andrew Eagle, and Debosmita Nandy for their valuable time and suggestions during the writing of this book. I am grateful to my editor Kimberley Lim and my publisher Jee Leong Koh for all their efforts in making my book a reality. Special thanks to Martin Pick and the University of East Anglia for giving me the opportunity to spend six months in Norwich and work on my novel.

Sheikh Mujibur Rahman's *The Unfinished Memoirs* and Akhtaruzzaman Elias's *Chilekothar Sepai* (Sepoy of the Attic) were among my favorite reads throughout the writing process. I owe them so much.

ABOUT THE AUTHOR

© Martin Pick

RAHAD ABIR is a writer from Bangladesh. His work has appeared in *Prairie Schooner, Witness, The Los Angeles Review, Himal Southasian, Courrier International, The Wire,* and elsewhere. He has an MFA in Fiction from Boston University. He is the recipient of the Charles Pick Fellowship at the University of East Anglia and the Marguerite McGlinn Prize for Fiction. His work has been translated into French and Hindi. Currently he is working on a short story collection, which was a finalist for the 2021 Miami Book Fair Emerging Writer Fellowship. He lives in Georgia, USA.

ABOUT

GAUDY BOY

From the Latin *gaudium*, meaning "joy," Gaudy Boy publishes books that delight readers with the various powers of art. The name is taken from the poem "Gaudy Turnout," by Singaporean poet Arthur Yap, about his time abroad in Leeds, the United Kingdom. Similarly inspired by such diasporic wanderings and migrations, Gaudy Boy brings literary works by authors of Asian heritage to the attention of an American audience and beyond. Established in 2018 as the imprint of the New York City–based literary nonprofit Singapore Unbound, we publish poetry, fiction, and literary nonfiction.

Visit our website at www.singaporeunbound.org/gaudyboy.

Winners of the Gaudy Boy Poetry Book Prize

Waking Up to the Pattern Left By a Snail Overnight, by Jim Pascual Agustin

Time Regime, by Jhani Randhawa

Object Permanence, by Nica Bengzon

Play for Time, by Paula Mendoza

Autobiography of Horse, by Jenifer Sang Eun Park

The Experiment of the Tropics, by Lawrence Lacambra Ypil

Fiction and Nonfiction

Picking off new shoots will not stop the spring, edited by Ko Ko Thett and Brian Haman

The Infinite Library and Other Stories, by Victor Fernando R. Ocampo

The Sweetest Fruits, by Monique Truong

And the Walls Come Crumbling Down, by Tania De Rozario

The Foley Artist, by Ricco Villanueva Siasoco

Malay Sketches, by Alfian Sa'at

From Gaudy Boy Translates

Amanat, edited by Zaure Batayeva and Shelley Fairweather-Vega

Ulirát, edited by Tilde Acuña, John Bengan, Daryll Delgado, Amado Anthony G. Mendoza III, and Kristine Ong Muslim

Other Series

New Singapore Poetries, edited by Marylyn Tan and Jee Leong Koh

Suspect: Volume 1, Year 1, edited by Jee Leong Koh

Printed in the USA
CPSIA information can be obtained
at www.ICGtesting.com
LVHW040804060923
757193LV00006B/112

9 781958 652022